I0570515

Pride Publishing books by L.M. Somerton

Single Books
Mountain Rescue
Black Dog
The Portrait
Stroke Rate
Chemical Bonds
Testing Lysander
Owned by the Sea

The Wyverns
Mantrap
Deathtrap
Rattrap
Sand Trap
Steel Trap

Tales from The Edge
Reaching the Edge
Living on the Edge
Dancing on the Edge
A Double-Edged Sword
Rough Around the Edges
Scorched Edges
Driven to the Edge
Binding the Edges

Investigating Love
Rasputin's Kiss
Evil's Embrace
Tarot's Love

Warlocks
Elemental Love
Elemental Hope
Elemental Faith

The Retreat
Serving Him
Trusting Him

Fairground Attractions
Ghost Train
Merry-Go-Round
Helter Skelter

Treasure Trove Antiques
The Lucky Cat

Anthologies
Racing Hearts: Keeping the Luck
His Rules: Tagging Mackenzie

Pride Publishing books by Cheryl Dragon

Single Books
One Weekend
Runaway Cowgirl

How to Catch a Cowboy
The Long Ride

Anthologies
Out of Bounds: Making the Pass

Pride Publishing books by Elizabeth Hollows

Single Books
Return to Duty

HARD EVIDENCE

Secret's Hold

Under His Protection

Ticket to Freedom

L.M. SOMERTON,
CHERYL DRAGON &
ELZABETH HOLLOWS

Hard Evidence
ISBN # 978-1-83943-916-2
©Copyright L.M. Somerton, Cheryl Dragon & Elizabeth Hollows 2020
Cover Art by Claire Siemaszkiewicz ©Copyright September 2020
Interior text design by Claire Siemaszkiewicz
Pride Publishing

This is a work of fiction. All characters, places and events are from the author's imagination and should not be confused with fact. Any resemblance to persons, living or dead, events or places is purely coincidental.

All rights reserved. No part of this publication may be reproduced in any material form, whether by printing, photocopying, scanning or otherwise without the written permission of the publisher, Pride Publishing.

Applications should be addressed in the first instance, in writing, to Pride Publishing. Unauthorised or restricted acts in relation to this publication may result in civil proceedings and/or criminal prosecution.

The author and illustrator have asserted their respective rights under the Copyright Designs and Patents Acts 1988 (as amended) to be identified as the author of this book and illustrator of the artwork.

Published in 2020 by Pride Publishing, United Kingdom.

No part of this book may be reproduced, scanned, or distributed in any printed or electronic form without permission. Please do not participate in or encourage piracy of copyrighted materials in violation of the authors' rights. Purchase only authorised copies.

Pride Publishing is an imprint of Totally Entwined Group Limited.

If you purchased this book without a cover you should be aware that this book is stolen property. It was reported as "unsold and destroyed" to the publisher and neither the author nor the publisher has received any payment for this "stripped book".

SECRET'S HOLD

L.M. SOMERTON

Chapter One

As always, I walked the half-mile from my small apartment to Spikes, the club where I'd worked six days a week for the last five months. It didn't get any easier, but fear and revulsion had dulled to self-pitying resignation. In my mind it was a game. Every day I climbed the ladder of success as I survived another shift, only to descend the greasy pole to get deposited back at Spikes' staff entrance the next night. Five months of hiding. Five months of pretending to be someone, something, I was not. I paused opposite the entrance to the club and resisted the urge to check the shadows. I needed to work, and the one positive of being employed at Spikes was that I could earn good money and still stay off official radars.

Down the dingy side alley that ran the length of the building, Robbie stood guard at the back door. Most of the staff called him Bubba, but to me he was Robbie. I crossed the road then glanced up at him. He was stern and forbidding, but there was always a twinkle in his dark eyes for me.

"Behave yourself tonight, Jamie. I don't want to be extricating your pretty little arse from another fight."

I switched on my trademark cheeky grin as I slipped past him. "Is it my fault that the punters get excited around me?"

He tried to give me a clip around the ear but missed—deliberately, I thought. I experienced a little pang of regret. He was just my type—big, hairy and fierce. In another life I would have flirted with him, but I couldn't afford too much attention, and a relationship of any kind was out of the question.

I trudged across the club, pushed through the staffroom door then changed into my working uniform of black leather trousers and a skin-tight latex top. The outfit no longer made me want to hide behind the nearest pillar, but I hated the pawing and groping that it attracted.

As the other guys changed around me, banging their locker doors and chattering about football, I felt so alone. If I'd had broader shoulders, I would have squared them. As it was, I just pushed my slight frame upright, fixed a grin on my face and walked into the cavernous bar, remembering just in time to add a mischievous wiggle to my hips.

"Jamie, you're fucking late. This isn't a bloody tea room."

I gave Ellis, my boss, the finger and sat on the edge of a table, swinging my legs and trying to look as bored as possible.

"For that, you get section six as well as your own. We're one short tonight. Enjoy."

Power had gone to Ellis' ginger head. Promoted one day and he'd already turned into an arsehole. I stuck my tongue out at him as soon as his back was turned, but inside I was groaning. Tonight was *not* going to be fun.

The staff briefing was short and to the point. Once the club opened, covering two sections proved virtually impossible and I had to run to keep up with the orders. The punters loved watching the sweat gleam on my arms and face. One guy even tried to lick me. The masochist who had designed the Spikes uniform got some extra-special cursing as wet latex clung to my body and chafed my skin. I was sticky with heat and spilt booze, my hair damp against my face. Bruises from stray elbows and table corners ached beneath leather trousers too hot to endure.

Muscles protesting, I unloaded a tray of drinks for the raucous crowd in a corner booth, avoiding eye contact and ignoring their crude remarks. Leather chaps and a studded jock strap might look good on some men, but the bloke sporting the outfit was built like the proverbial brick outhouse, and the gear didn't really suit him. I cringed as he grabbed my wrist and forced me to straddle his thighs. I was held from behind and rough hands pushed my legs farther apart, giving him access to my fly. He licked his lips and grinned while he grasped my zip with meaty fingers, ignoring my struggles and protests.

"Get the fuck off of me! You do *not* tip well enough for this!"

"Mm-m. Resist all you like, blondie. You're not going anywhere."

There was no room for underwear beneath my uniform trousers, which didn't normally bother me.

Tonight, I would have happily slipped into a pair of cast-iron Y-fronts, because the arsehole's goons gripped my arms tighter as he yanked my trousers down to my thighs. They twisted me across his lap and I forced my head around so that I didn't have to look at his leather-clad bulge. I screamed as his hand connected with my arse, leaving a burning trail across my skin. He bent his head close to my ear, and beer-sour breath filled my nostrils as he wound a hand into my hair and dragged my head up.

"I'm going to fuck you so hard that you'll never walk again."

The whispered words made me fight and struggle even more, but he just laughed. His cronies jeered and urged him on as I was forced facedown onto the padded bench and held there by a collection of willing hands. I caught one glimpse of a huge, purple-veined cock as he moved behind me, and my mind went blank, my body limp.

Then there was an ear-splitting scream and it hadn't come from me. Robbie threw my attacker across a table and into the nearest wall with one effortless heave. Fists flying, he cleared the area in seconds and hauled me to my feet.

"Get into the staff room and sort yourself out."

I didn't need telling twice. I yanked up my trousers then ran, leaving the chaos behind me. The dingy room felt as good as any holy sanctuary—quiet and empty. I stripped off my shirt then toweled the sweat from my neck and chest. A dousing under the cold tap shocked me back to reality as I raked my shaking hands through dripping hair. My heart pounded when the door opened, but it was just Robbie checking up on me. His look of concern was replaced by something else as he took in my bare chest.

"Okay?" Robbie was a man of few words.

I nodded with a confidence I didn't feel. "Sure. Just give me a minute."

He frowned. "Take ten. You're voted in for the lockdown, so you may as well change and take a breather."

I sighed. Punters paid extra for the after-hours lockdown and voted for the waitstaff they wanted to serve them. It was the last thing I needed. Robbie looked like he was going to say something else but turned away and closed the door behind him. I slumped against the wall and made a heroic effort to hold back my tears. I didn't deserve any of this. One stupid decision, one moment's curiosity, shouldn't mean my life had to be this miserable.

"Suck it up, J." *How about those for inspirational words of self-motivation?* I stripped completely and let the air caress my body for a moment before pulling on tight leather shorts. They were indecent, barely covering the curve of my arse and riding low on my hips. My fingers had steadied enough to fasten the collar around my neck and I twisted it so that the attached lead hung down my back. I turned short white socks over the top of my black combat boots and resisted the urge to count the bruises blooming on my pale skin.

I drank half a bottle of cold water and took a few slow, calming breaths. "You can do this. Just blank it out." I pushed the door open and peered into the club. It was the biggest lockdown crowd I'd ever seen. My eyes roamed across the sea of men—some familiar, some fresh. Then my gaze rested on a face I knew—not a regular punter, but someone from my past.

"Fuck!" The feeling of panic far surpassed the fear I'd felt at the prospect of rape. My vision blurred, and I couldn't think straight. I had to get out. I shot across the bar, barreling through the exit into the street. I caught one brief look at Robbie's startled face, then turned…straight into the path of an oncoming van.

* * * *

I woke up in a hospital bed. Usually, when I come out of a really deep sleep, there's a slow recognition of familiar surroundings, followed by an overwhelming urge to turn over and sink back into warm darkness. This was the opposite. My eyes snapped open to the off-white glare of strip lighting, the stabbing knife of panic in my guts and a desperate need to run. *But run from what? To where?* I had no fucking idea. It was impossible anyway. I'd sat up way too fast, and the room swam. A dull throb at the base of my skull kept time with my pulse and I lifted shaking fingers to touch the dressing taped to the back of my neck.

I slumped back onto my pillows, squeezing my eyes shut against the pain and took deep breaths of sterile, disinfectant-scented air. Gradually the nausea subsided, and I opened my eyes again, just a crack. Through the bars of my lashes, I could see a green, vinyl-upholstered armchair in one corner of the room. Next to the bed was a cupboard on wheels. There was a covered jug on the top and a plastic cup. Water seemed like a good idea, so I poured a drink then sipped it slowly. The moisture on my dry throat and tongue was good, and I wondered how long it had been since I had drunk anything. I was shirtless, one of my arms was grazed and bruised, but nothing seemed to be broken. I took an uneasy peek beneath the bed covers and discovered a pair of blue cotton scrub pants covering my slim and apparently undamaged legs.

There was a plastic nametag around my left wrist that read Jamie Ackerton-Mills. The name meant nothing, even though I repeated it over and over in the hope that something would register. The window was covered with a half-closed blind. It was light outside — if dull and gray — and it felt like morning, though I had no evidence that was the case until the door clicked open and a nurse walked in with a cheery, "Good morning! Finally awake, I see."

Another jolt of panic hit me, and I scrambled to sit up. *Big mistake.* The nausea returned with a vengeance. The nurse was quick. I'd give her that. A cardboard bowl was thrust beneath my chin and a gentle arm encircled my shoulders as I revisited my last meal.

"There there, sweetie. Is that better?"

"Sorry," I mumbled into the cup of water that she placed in my shaking hand and guided to my mouth. "How long have I been here?"

She brushed strands of hair away from my eyes. "Since last night. Just relax, honey. I'll fetch the doctor." She plumped my pillows so that I could sit up then bustled away.

So, this was a hospital and I had been in some kind of accident that had left me unconscious for... I didn't know how long. Carefully, so as not to jolt anything important, I swiveled out of bed. My bare feet made contact with the cold vinyl floor and I balanced myself with a hand on the bed as I adjusted to being upright. I could remember how to walk. I gave myself a mental pat on the back for that and headed toward the small en suite.

I avoided looking in the mirror until I'd washed my hands and splashed cold water on my face. I gathered my courage and looked up slowly. The stranger who stared back at me gave a small, sardonic smile. Bedhead was a major understatement. My light blond hair looked as if an entire tribe of monkeys had been playing Twister in it. It was quite long on top, shorter around my ears and was sticking out in every possible direction. Puzzled brown eyes looked back at me as I examined my girlish features, Cupid's-bow lips and small nose. My slightly pointed chin was covered in golden fuzz that didn't qualify as stubble. I was pretty. There was no denying it. Not ruggedly handsome... pretty—the kind of boy that old ladies liked to pat on the head and call 'angel'. I wasn't feeling very fucking angelic.

Judging from my reflection, I was about five feet nine. I wasn't sporting a six-pack, but I was quite nicely toned. I looked carefully, but there was no sign of a single hair on my chest and a peek down under showed little more than a triangle of golden fluff. I wasn't exactly packing heavy hardware down there either, but it was a decent mouthful. *Where did that thought come from?* I pictured a man on his knees, sucking contentedly. *Being gay isn't something that disappears with amnesia, then. Someone could probably write a scientific paper about that.*

I used the john, washed up again and meandered from the en suite, across my room, to a window to look for a clue as to where the hell I was. I could see an elevated road straddling low sheds and warehouses. Older buildings huddled together against the encroaching steel and glass of modern office blocks. It all seemed familiar, but there was nothing specific that could identify exactly which city it was. I shrugged and headed back to my bed, pausing to take a quick look in the cupboard next to it. Apart from a Bible and a couple of ancient gardening magazines, it was empty.

Back in the haven of my bed, I pulled the covers up to my chin to allay the shivering that had taken over my body. I think it was shock more than cold, a delayed reaction to discovering the fog in my mind and the confusion that came with it. My name meant nothing to me and I couldn't remember anything about my past. I slumped back onto the pillows with a sigh and closed my eyes.

I must have drifted back to sleep, but the sound of the door opening pulled the trigger on my eyelids. The nurse I had met earlier came into the room, accompanied by a gray-haired woman in a white coat with a stethoscope around her neck.

"How are you feeling, Jamie? I understand you were a little sick earlier?" The doctor didn't wait for me to respond. "That's only to be expected after a bump on the head." She scribbled something on the chart that had been hanging on the end of my bed. She breathed on the cold metal end of her stethoscope before pressing it against my chest. After a few seconds, she pulled the earpieces out, slung the instrument around her neck and smiled. "That sounds fine. You're healthy as a horse."

I scowled. "How can I be all right when I can't remember who I am? You call me Jamie and I've read the nametag around my wrist, but how do you know that's my name?"

"A colleague came in the ambulance with you. He gave us your details. I'm sure he'll be back later. In the meantime, try not to worry. The scan we gave you shows no problem with your brain. Your memory will return in time." She gave me a reassuring smile.

"How long will it take?"

"There's no way of knowing, I'm afraid. It could be a few hours, days or even weeks. I'm not a betting girl, but I'd put money on no more than a couple of days. You have a cut and bruising at the base of your skull and some grazing on your arm. You'll be stiff for a few days, so I would suggest you avoid dancing for a while." She snickered.

I had no idea why she found that statement funny.

"We've had the clothes that you arrived in cleaned up, though you may want to wait for your friend to bring you something more...suitable to wear before you go home."

"I don't understand."

She patted my shoulder then went to the door. "You will." She smiled. "You can go home as soon as you're ready. Make sure you complete the paperwork at the nurses' station on the way out."

I have so many questions and she's just going to leave? "Wait! You haven't told me what happened. How did I get here?"

The doctor paused. "I only have the story second-hand from the paramedics, but apparently you ran into the road and came off second best in an argument with a van. Someone called an ambulance and the paramedics scraped you off the tarmac. That was last night and you've been unconscious ever since. Consider yourself lucky. It could have been much worse."

She left with a wave that seemed far too casual. The nurse left briefly then returned with a trolley holding a plate of sandwiches and a bowl of chocolate mousse. I smiled at that, happy to see that hospital food lived up to its reputation. Also, I loved chocolate. *I wonder how I know that.*

My folded clothes sat on the bottom of the trolley. As soon as the nurse had gone, I got out of the bed and picked up the small pile. Laying the garments out on the bed, I swallowed. I didn't remember what I did for a living, but it seemed that I did it wearing nothing but black leather shorts and a collar.

"Oh. My. God." I sat on the edge of the bed with my head in my hands. I definitely couldn't leave the hospital wearing those clothes. The shorts looked like they would barely cover my arse. I fingered the leather collar and the lead attached to it and tried desperately to remember something, anything, that would give me a clue as to who I was.

I ate the dry sandwiches then spooned down the mousse. I flicked through the gardening magazines before spending some time in the small bathroom, having a proper wash and shave. When I came out, still scrubbing my face with a towel, the room seemed darker.

"Hi, Jamie, it's good to see you awake."

I turned toward the voice and realized that a huge man blocking the entire door was causing the eclipse. He had to be six feet six. Tattooed, muscled arms stuck out of his black T-shirt. In fact, his entire body seemed to be one slab of muscle. Collar-length hair and a short beard matched the dark fur that coated his arms.

I took a couple of involuntary steps backward. This guy was scary. His fierce expression softened. "It's okay, Jamie. I've brought your clothes from the club and I've got the bike outside. The doc says I can take you home when you're ready."

"Who are you?" Fear laced my words with acid, but he just gave me an indulgent smile.

"I'm Bubba. I'm a bouncer at Spikes, the club you work at."

I held out my hands for the bag he was carrying. "Thanks for bringing my clothes. My working wardrobe is apparently not appropriate for everyday use."

Bubba grinned. "But you look damned hot in it."

My face heated, and I lowered my eyes in embarrassment. What was worse, my cock was also swelling at his words. I looked at him again and caught a strange expression passing across his face. It was a combination of lust and gentle humor, combined with a glint in his eye that suggested he knew exactly how my body was responding to him.

I took my clothes into the bathroom then closed the door. The clothes he'd brought me were reassuringly normal. There was no underwear in the bag, so I just pulled on the jeans and loose cotton shirt. I left the scrub trousers hanging on the towel rail and returned to the room. Bubba was sitting on the edge of my bed, thumbing through one of the discarded magazines.

"There weren't any shoes in your locker at the club, so I hoped you'd be able to wear the boots you had on when you decided to pick a fight with that van."

I scowled and laced the black combat boots quickly then stuffed my other clothes into the now-empty bag. I raked my fingers through my hair, trying to bring it to some semblance of order, and took a deep breath. "Thanks for coming, Bubba. I hope you know where I live, because that's something else I can't remember." He'd brought me my watch, wallet and a bunch of keys. There were two ten-pound notes in the wallet but nothing with an address on it. I felt helpless and frustrated.

By the time I'd received instructions on how to change my dressing, filled in what seemed like reams of paperwork with Bubba's help and picked up some medication from the pharmacy, it was early afternoon. I stood next to Bubba in the lift, queasy and very insecure. He didn't speak much. *Clearly the strong, silent type.* I smiled to myself and cast surreptitious glances in his direction. I could smell the leather of his jacket and the warm, spicy scent of whatever he had used in the shower that morning. The thought of him naked in the shower caused my cock to stiffen yet again. Mentally I cursed hormones too young to know any better and shifted my weight from one foot to the other in a vain attempt to make myself more comfortable. When we reached the ground floor, people spewed out onto the concourse. I had to get some air.

"Are you okay?" Bubba felt my forehead with his enormous hand. "You're very warm."

"I'm fine." I backed away from his touch. "I need to get outside. The smell of this place is making me sick."

He moved his hand to the small of my back and gently propelled me toward the sliding glass doors. Despite the diesel fumes from idling ambulances, I sucked in a lungful of air. Everything seemed vaguely familiar, and that was comforting in a way, but there was still a sensation of fear in the pit of my stomach that wouldn't go away.

"Is something wrong?" Bubba asked. "You look like someone expecting to get mugged."

"I don't know," I replied. "I just feel…like something bad is going to happen, but I can't tell you why."

"Nothing is going to happen to you while I'm around." Bubba spoke with absolute certainty. "Let's get you home. Being surrounded by familiar things might help you remember stuff."

I nodded and trailed behind him into the lower deck of the nearby car park. His bike was propped on its axle stand in one corner, a mass of gleaming black metal and chrome. Bubba unlocked the box on the back of the bike and pulled out two helmets and a leather jacket. "I brought a spare kit for you that my sister uses sometimes. I think it should fit."

"Your sister?"

He chuckled at my indignation. "She's a big girl."

The helmet and the jacket fit fine. I straddled the bike behind Bubba and wrapped my arms around him. He felt so good. Even through the leather of his jacket, I could feel his muscles flexing as he manipulated the throttle. The purr of the powerful engine sent vibrations through my body and I had to suppress a moan as my still-stiff cock was subjected to unavoidable stimulation.

The journey was short but exhilarating. I thought I would be scared of the bike's speed and power, but Bubba was solid as a rock in front of me and that gave me confidence. It took less than fifteen minutes of weaving through the traffic before Bubba pulled over. He turned off the engine in front of a converted warehouse.

I scrambled off the bike with little grace and stood on the pavement, my thigh muscles trembling. Bubba swung a long leg across the saddle and held out his hand for my helmet. He stored it and his own in the box on the back of the bike then pointed at the building. "This is where you live. Does it look familiar at all?"

I gazed up at three forbidding stories. It could have been a detention center or a slaughterhouse. There was no spark of recognition for the dull gray stone or the rows of glinting windows. I'd like to be able to say they looked like eyes, but that would suggest the building had personality, when it was one amorphous mass of brick and metal. I shook my head in bewilderment but pulled the bunch of keys from my pocket and took a couple of faltering steps toward the door. Bubba gripped my shoulder with a large hand.

"I'll come with you. It might be different once you get inside your own place."

The steel doors at the front of the building led to a communal hallway. There was an old-fashioned cage elevator going up through the center of the building but I rejected it in favor of the stairs, because it was like Hammer horror movie scenery and no doubt contained ghosts, or monsters or both.

The stairwell was dark and smelled like it had been swabbed down with bleach, but it could have been worse. Bubba and I trudged up to the top floor, me regretting not taking the lift, however scary, and we walked to the end of a dim corridor. The number on my door was six, and to my relief, the biggest key on my ring released the lock. Bubba pushed the door open for me and gestured for me to go inside.

There was a small hallway, and I could see several doors leading off it. The first was a closet, the second a small shower room. The next led to a scene of utter devastation. It was as if a tornado had ripped through what used to be a lounge or dining room. Broken furniture was strewn everywhere. It was difficult to see the floor because there was so much debris. I stood in the doorway and blinked, unable to take in the scene in front of me. I walked to the only remaining door down the hall and looked in on similar wreckage. My bedroom looked as if something with huge claws had been sharpening its talons on every available surface. The curtains and bedding were shredded, the bed upturned and the doors of the wardrobe were smashed on the floor.

I leaned against the wall and slid down it until my arse hit the floor. I put my head in my hands. I was either the messiest guy on the planet or someone had ransacked my home while I had been in the hospital. My accident and this invasion had to be connected. I was utterly lost and it was all I could do not to cry.

"I don't know what you've got yourself into, kid, but you can't stay here. We should call the police, then you can come back to my place." Bubba hauled me to my feet as if I weighed nothing.

"No! No police!" I knew with absolute certainty that involving the authorities would be a mistake. I just didn't know why. "There's no need for you to stay, Bubba. This isn't your problem. I'll clear a space and crash. I'll worry about cleaning up in the morning."

Bubba growled. It was the kind of sound that a grizzly bear, disturbed too early from hibernation, might make. "Unless you want my hand across your arse, you'll do as you're told. Now grab some things — if there's anything left worth grabbing — and move."

I thought about refusing for all of five seconds. Bubba seemed like the type who would deliver exactly what he promised, and I'd had enough trauma for one day. Amid the detritus of my excuse for a life, I managed to salvage some underwear, socks, a couple of T-shirts, jeans and an ancient sweater. Bubba propelled me out of the door. It seemed pointless to lock it but I did anyway.

"How did they get in, Bubba? The front door wasn't damaged."

He shrugged. "Looks more like a message than a burglary to me, and there's ways and means of getting through a door that don't involve battering rams."

Bubba's place was twenty minutes away on the bike. When he parked and the bike's low rumble died away, I felt dizzy and sick. It must have showed when I pulled off the helmet, because Bubba took one look at me, swore softly and put a supporting arm around my trembling shoulders.

My flickering eyelids gave me strobe-like impressions of blood-red roses, lustrous brass against a deep blue door, then the warm golden glow of wooden flooring. Bubba half pushed, half-carried me up the stairs into a haven of cool green and white. He stripped me, but I didn't have the energy to react as his large hands brushed my skin. The contrast between us couldn't have been more extreme—my smooth, pale skin and light blond hair against Bubba's weather-beaten tan and dark beard. My slight form seemed fragile compared to the solidity of his powerful frame. My last impressions through the pain of a pounding headache were of cobalt and burgundy designs dancing on his skin as his arm muscles flexed, and he placed me gently into bed. I think he stood there watching me for a while, but I couldn't say for certain. I only know that I slept a dreamless sleep, secure in the knowledge of his presence.

Chapter Two

Morning brought consciousness and a tidal wave of memories that crashed over me with terrifying force. I remembered everything and it was overwhelming. The who, what and why of my life pummeled my senses into numb submission. Amnesia suddenly didn't seem so bad. A lot of my recent memories would be better off consigned to darkness.

Trembling in reaction, I spotted the open door to an en suite bathroom and made it to the sink before the ominous tightening of my throat turned into uncontrollable vomiting. The acid burn in my mouth diminished as I rinsed, spat and swallowed cool water from the tap. I braced my arms against the porcelain to steady myself. There was a light tap on the door, and I turned to Bubba's stoic gaze. Suddenly shy, I covered myself with my hands.

"How are you feeling?"

The man wants conversation, now? I rolled my eyes, grabbed a towel to preserve a modicum of decency then retreated to the defense of sarcasm. "Just fucking peachy, thanks. I love to revisit my last meal first thing in the morning, Robbie." That gave it away. Using his real name rather than his nickname brought a grin to his hairy face.

"You're back, then?"

I nodded. I didn't want to answer his questions yet, and he seemed to sense my reticence. "Take a shower. I'll start some breakfast." He turned away. "We *are* going to talk, Jamie, so get ready to share the burden. I've got broad shoulders. I can take the weight."

Showered, shaved and dressed in my rescued clothes, I padded barefoot down the stairs. I'd towel-dried my hair and left it deliberately messy — part of the disguise. I fixed a grin that I didn't mean on my face and went to find the kitchen. Robbie's house exuded good taste from every corner and I made a mental note to scrap all preconceptions about him from now on. I felt like I could trust him and I knew he looked after me at work. *Work... Jesus.* That memory had come with a healthy dose of angst.

The smell of crisping bacon drew me to the kitchen and a stool next to a cream marble counter. My stomach was grumbling, and despite my earlier sickness, I was starving. Robbie loaded a plate and put it in front of me.

"Eat. You look like a mild breeze would blow you over."

I gave him an indignant look. It was all right for him. A category five hurricane wouldn't stand a chance of moving the man. He stared coolly back, and I opted for the escape of a mouthful of eggs. He let me eat, but eventually, I had to push the empty plate away and face the interrogation from his eyes.

"So, I think you owe me the courtesy of your real name, don't you?"

I winced. "How did you know?"

"It was obvious. Yesterday at the hospital, your accent was different. Your cheeky brat personality had gone and you were shocked by your club clothes. It all added up to someone living a lie."

I ran a nervous hand through my damp hair. "Anything I tell you puts you at risk, Robbie. I'm in a lot of trouble. I saw something I shouldn't have and I think it's catching up with me."

Silence stretched between us. Robbie folded his arms and pressed his lips together in a tight line. I swallowed, feeling like a naughty schoolboy in front of the headmaster.

"Jay. My real name is Jay. I chose Jamie because it was close enough to my true name that I thought I wouldn't get caught out. If I said Jay by mistake, I could pass it off as an abbreviation."

"How on earth did you end up at Spikes? There must be easier places to bury yourself."

"Hide in plain sight. That was the idea, to go somewhere that no one would think of looking for me. Spikes is about as far from reality as it was possible for me to get. But the other night I thought I caught a glimpse of someone at the lockdown—someone who would have recognized me. There was no way I could stay, so I bolted. I was so busy looking over my shoulder that... Well, you know what happened next better than I do. I don't remember anything after running out of the club until I woke up at the hospital. That bang on the head wiped out my acting abilities and I suppose I reverted to the normal me. I just couldn't remember who that was."

"The *normal* you? There is nothing normal about you, Jay. You're either incredibly brave or utterly stupid."

The stool I was perched on began to feel a bit like a small island in shark-infested waters as Robbie paced with a grim look on his face. His plain black T-shirt was clinging in all the right places, and against all sensible odds, I began to get pleasantly distracted. I watched the dragon tattoo on his forearm, mesmerized by the way its tail seemed to twitch with every muscle flex. I ran my tongue along my lips. They were a poor substitute for where I'd have liked to have run it. I realized too late that Robbie had stopped pacing. *Caught in the act. Fuck.*

"If I'm going to help you, Jay, you need to focus."

Robbie looked like he wanted to give me a clip around the ear—or maybe kiss some sense into me. I preferred the latter option, but got the first. If he'd really hit me, I would have fallen off the stool. As it was, the flick to my earlobe stung enough to enforce his point, nothing more.

"Ow!" I rubbed at the sore spot and pouted.

Maybe he caught a glint in my eye, but suddenly I was pulled off the stool and into a crushing hug. I'd thought the armor I'd built was impregnable, but that simple act of caring found a chink and widened it as inexorably as frost attacking cracks in the pavement. Wrapped in warmth, squeezed by powerful muscle, I took a shuddering breath and managed not to cry.

Bubba stroked my hair then rested his huge hand over the dressing on the nape of my neck. I tilted my head back and gazed into his dark eyes. It would be so good to have someone to share this burden with, but I was loath to involve anyone else in my problems, especially Robbie. He must have sensed my reluctance, because he picked me up and put me firmly back on the stool.

"You don't move until you've told me everything, Jay." I parted my lips to protest but he pressed his finger against them. "Don't. You've carried this alone for months. It's time to share."

I sat there with my mouth clamped shut. Robbie leaned against the counter and smiled implacably. God, he looked sexy, all stern and tough. I could feel the heat growing at my groin and I moaned, sure that he would see the growing bulge in my jeans. I held my nerve for all of a minute. I tried to avoid the eyes drilling into me, but they followed my every twitch and fidget. It was no good. I would have to tell him.

Decision made, it felt like a massive weight was lifting from my shoulders before I'd uttered a word. "Okay. You win. I'll tell you everything, but can we please go somewhere more comfortable? And could you take the dressing off for me? It's pulling at my skin."

He eased the sticky edges away. "I think this will be okay uncovered. There's only a small cut and it's already healing. The bruising's nasty, though."

We relocated to the lounge, and I curled into the soft leather of a squishy armchair, tucking my bare feet beneath me. Robbie leaned against the doorframe.

I closed my eyes, allowing my mind to drift backward and pick the moment to start my story. I squinted then removed a pair of colored contact lenses and regarded Robbie with my true eyes. My mother had always told me that they were my best feature — *'the color of bluebells in spring,'* she would say.

"My name is Jay Medlicott. I'm twenty, the only son of Giles Medlicott…" I waited to see if Robbie recognized the name.

"Medlicott Industries? The arms manufacturer?"

I nodded. Anyone would have to have been dead for the last ten years not to have heard about the massive contracts my dad's company had won from several governments around the world.

"I've been at university for the last two years and had gone home for the summer. It was something my father had insisted on." He had always been strict, but in his own brusque way, he loved me. "I was bored…lonely. I came out to my parents when I was eighteen and they were very tolerant, but when I was at home, my father wouldn't allow me to socialize anywhere that I might be photographed, especially with another man. He's very protective of his privacy. Anyway, I know it makes me sound like a spoiled brat, but I snuck out one night and went to the kind of club that Daddy Dearest would have disapproved of the most. I thought it would be safe. They were having a masked ball theme night, so I could cover my face and remain anonymous. It was just supposed to be a bit of fun…"

I frowned and massaged my temples, trying to soothe the ache of tension. "It was dark, hot and crowded. There must have been three hundred people, but the atmosphere was friendly. I was careful, never talking to the same guy for long. I danced for a while and it got really hot, so I took a bottle of water outside to cool off. I leaned on the railings at the front of the place and tried to make out the constellations. I was about to go back inside when I heard this noise, like a cat squealing, from the side alley. I went to look…"

Robbie grunted and I squirmed in my chair. "I know! Unbelievably dumb, with the benefit of hindsight. Anyway, there were four guys down there. Two were keeping watch and another was leaning against the wall while some kid on his knees sucked him off. They were all wearing masks, and the kid didn't seem to be under duress. I turned to go, but then it all changed. Fists started flying, then the kid was on the floor getting a good kicking. I just watched, Robbie. I'm ashamed to admit it, but I was too scared to do anything. They went back into the club through the fire escape, leaving the boy on the ground. As the last one went in, he held the side of the door and the light caught a ring he was wearing—a big chunky thing shaped like a skull. He hesitated, as if he'd heard something, and I thought he'd seen me, but I drew back into the shadows. Then they were gone. I called an ambulance and left before it arrived. I couldn't risk anyone taking my name."

The shame was as real as it had been that night, warming my cheeks with the burn of regret. I let my hair fall over my eyes and hid behind the blond curtain, not wanting to see judgement on Robbie's face.

"It was a nasty experience, Jay, but none of this explains why you're hiding out here. Tell me the rest."

"I went home to bed and tried to forget what I'd seen, but a couple of days later there was a newspaper report. The boy outside the club had died. I'd witnessed a murder and I was in a no-win situation. If I went to the police, I'd be exposing myself to the killer and letting down my father. If I stayed quiet, I didn't think I'd be able to live with the guilt." I paused and Robbie gave me an encouraging look. "I spent a whole day locked in my bedroom, worrying about what to do, but

I suppose there was only ever going to be one solution, and that was to report what I'd seen.

"I decided to go to the police the next morning, but in the meantime, I had to get through a formal dinner with my parents and some business guests. I tried to get out of it by pretending to be tired, saying that I had a headache, but my father gave me one of his special looks that promised to make my life miserable if I didn't show up and play the dutiful son, so I did my bit. I changed into a shirt and tie and showed up for pre-dinner drinks. As well as my parents, there were three other couples there and they were all pleasant company, but when we went in for dinner, there was still a seat that remained empty. I remember that my father made some comment that *Andrew* always liked to make a grand entrance—Andrew Urquhart, the MP and a rising star in the Ministry of Defense.

"Anyway, we had started the first course when he finally arrived. The empty seat was to my right, so I was interested in seeing the man who I was going to have to make polite conversation with. He and my father could have been formed from the same mold—expensive suit, discreet Rolex, old school tie. He was tan and his teeth had seen some expensive dentistry. He was the whole package—rich, powerful. I hate to admit it, but he had the makings of the next Prime Minister and the connections to make it happen.

"Introductions made, he sat down beside me. He was one of those men who felt the need to assert his dominance through a crushing handshake, and I could feel metal digging into my fingers. I suppose you can guess what I saw when I looked down? His ring... It was a hideous gold monstrosity in the shape of a skull with red-jeweled eyes.

31

"I was so shocked that I couldn't mask my expression in time. I knew instantly that he realized his ring meant something to me. I must have gone white, because my mother turned to me and asked if I was feeling okay. I used her concern as a shield, made my excuses and left the table. When I got back to my room, I was shaking, and it took me a good while to calm down and think about what to do. Urquhart was— No, *is* a powerful man with violent friends, and he wouldn't hesitate to take desperate measures to protect himself. I didn't think my family would be at risk. Urquhart needed my father and Dad knew nothing of what I'd seen.

"I got no sleep that night. My father left for work, and my mother went out to meet friends. I threw some clothes into a bag then headed for the station. I emptied my bank account and threw all my identification into a bin. Then I got on the first train south and ended up in Bristol." I fell silent, expecting scorn, judgment or, at the very least, another clip around the ear. Robbie walked over to the window and looked out in silent contemplation.

"So, let me get this straight. You ran to protect yourself. You've managed to stay hidden for five months by living in a dump and doing a job that you find degrading and humiliating. You've given up everything you knew and kept silent all this time?"

"All I saw was a ring. I didn't see his face, so I have no real evidence that Urquhart did anything wrong other than my own gut instinct that he was there that night. If I go to the police, my father's name gets dragged through the papers because his gay son witnessed some fag getting a bashing down a seedy back alley. No one is going to care, Robbie. No one but

Urquhart, and I think the robbery at my place shows that he hasn't given up on tidying up loose ends."

"I'm not criticizing, Jay. I'm amazed at how brave you've been."

"I'm not brave. I'm a coward. I should have reported what I saw straight away. Now it's too late, and there's no going back. I need to move on again before someone else gets hurt." Tears welled and I brushed them away. I didn't have time for crying. In fact, I made to stand. Robbie crossed the room then shoved me, gently, back into the chair.

"Sit."

"Robbie, you've been great, but I can't be near people I care about." Too late, I realized what I'd said and cast my eyes down.

"I care about you too, Jay." Robbie's voice was deep and gruff. It sent shivers of pleasure down my spine. "And that means we deal with this together." He tilted my chin up. "Don't even think about arguing."

In my mind I was begging him to lean closer and kiss me. I craved the contact of his lips against mine, and the need must have shown in my eyes. He gripped my chin firmly and, for a moment, I thought I saw the same desire in his expression, but it was fleeting.

"No. You're too vulnerable. I won't take advantage of your situation." He ruffled my hair then turned away.

Fuck. Every atom of my being screamed, *Take advantage! Now!* "I'm stronger than I look, I can take care of myself." Frustration gave my words a sharpness I didn't feel and I instantly regretted my tone. "I'm sorry. It's just that I've gotten used to being alone. No one has done anything nice for me in the last five months. At the club, a smile usually means a punter wants me on my knees."

"I want you to work tonight as usual." Robbie paused as if to gauge my reaction. "I'm going to call in a few favors, but we need to find out how close Urquhart is getting. Was there anything at your flat that might have given away where you work?"

"I don't think so." I thought hard. I always changed at Spikes, so my uniform was kept in my locker. I was paid in cash and tips, so there was no paperwork with the club's name on it. Then I groaned. "I had a matchbook in the kitchen, one of those free ones they keep in bowls on the bar."

"And the person you saw at Spikes, was it Urquhart?"

"No. It was one of the thugs who was with him the night the kid got hurt."

"I think we can assume that your place was broken into after you left for work on the day you had your accident. Do you think you were seen?"

"No. I'm certain I wasn't. I'd definitely not seen the guy in Spikes before, either."

"Okay. I have to go out for a while. I'll be back to take you to work."

I stood up. "You can't just disappear without telling me what you're up to, Robbie. I'm not some child you can lock in his room."

"Believe me, Jay. I don't see you as a child." The expression on his face made my cock jerk. "But it's best you don't know too much. You need to look sweet and innocent tonight."

"Why? I want to come with you…"

Robbie suddenly looked very fierce. "I don't want to lock you in, but I will if you can't give me your word that you'll stay put."

All the energy drained from my body. "Fine." I collapsed back into the chair, defeated.

"Try not to worry. I'll be back as soon as I can."

The house vibrated as Robbie fired up his bike and headed away. I started taking in the details of my surroundings for the first time. The house was beautiful. Soft, colorful rugs and drapes gave warmth to the neutral tones used on the walls. There was a wood burner in the lounge and a stunning copper-framed mirror above it. *Art nouveau...* It looked like a Liberty & Co. original and must have cost a fortune. I brushed my fingers along the beaten metal edge in appreciation. The carpets were soft beneath my bare feet as I padded from room to room, examining the expensive artwork, sculptures and extensive shelves of books.

The décor was masculine but not harsh. My small apartment could have fit into the kitchen and there were five large bedrooms upstairs. I felt ridiculously shy as I peeped around the door and found what was obviously Robbie's room, before pushing it wide. Cool white contrasted with the deepest green on one wall and a heavy quilt in the same shade that covered the king-size bed. All the furniture was antique, fashioned from golden oak and intricately carved. There was a large bathroom attached, glowing with modern chrome and white marble. I pulled open the wardrobe doors then fingered the clothes. Everything felt expensive, though there was a disproportionate amount of denim and leather. Robbie clearly had a great deal of wealth, concealed by good taste and a complete lack of ostentation.

I climbed onto his bed and lay sideways across it, luxuriating in the softness and the scent that lingered on the pillows. Not totally in control of my actions, I flicked open the stud of my jeans and slid the zip down. I grasped the warmth of my dormant cock with cool fingers. My imagination replaced fear and anxiety with images of Robbie stripping off his leathers. I'd only seen him dressed, but I was convinced his body would be magnificent. My hand moved slowly but my cock needed little prompting. Suddenly hot, I scrambled out of my clothes and lay naked across the dark covers. Bending my legs, I stroked my dick with one hand while seeking my entrance with the other.

I'd never had another man inside me, but I had no doubt it was what I wanted. I was burning inside, desperate to be filled. I moved my hand faster, heading inexorably toward an orgasm. I began to pant in short, sharp gasps as I ran my thumb over the sensitive head of my cock before jacking it with hard, uncoordinated movements. Globs of white spattered my thigh as I succumbed to a release that made me feel lonelier than I had at any time in the last five months.

I gave in to the pent-up emotion and wept. Huge, shuddering sobs racked my body as I tried and failed to get a grip. My defensive wall, always a little cracked and unstable, had finally crumbled. I cried until there were no more tears left. Shaking, I hauled myself into the shower in the hope that hot water would wash away some of the pain. Afterward, I did feel calmer, though it was the calm of resignation rather than resolution.

* * * *

When Robbie returned a few hours later, I was curled into a corner of the sofa reading a book. Though the puffiness around my eyes had subsided, I could tell from his frown that Robbie knew I had been crying. Mentioning it would have set me off again and he had the good judgement to keep quiet. Instead, he threw a leather jacket at me.

"Get your arse in gear. We're going out."

A fifteen-minute ride took us to an anonymous warehouse on an industrial estate. There was no signage, just an electronic keypad. Robbie punched in some numbers to release the door. There was A small lobby led to another security door with a discreet camera positioned above it. Robbie stared directly at the camera and the next door clicked open. He strolled through, and I followed, not nearly so assured. I was very aware of how little I knew about Robbie, and blind faith had never been one of my failings.

I'm not sure what I was expecting, but it wasn't the huge space that opened out before us. Dotted with supporting pillars, the area was split in two. On one side there were the mats and equipment one might find in a martial arts training facility. On the other was a well-equipped gym with an emphasis on free weights. There were several treadmills and rowing machines, but no bikes or StairMasters. There was no music playing or video screens flashing, just the sounds of intense physical effort.

A handsome young man, a little taller than me and probably in his mid-twenties, joined us. He wore shorts and a polo shirt in plain navy, no logos or insignia, and on peering around, I could see at least three other men wearing the same kit. They all seemed to be supervising or instructing, so it didn't take genius to work out they were staff.

"Afternoon, Boss." The man grinned. He gave me a curious look. "And this must be the famous Jamie?" He shook my hand. "You have no idea how long we've all been waiting to meet you."

Next to me, Robbie sighed. "Adam...you have all the subtlety of a charging fucking rhinoceros."

"Yes, Boss." Adam tried for contrite and failed miserably.

I stole a sideways glance at Robbie. I could have sworn he was pink underneath all that hair. *Is he blushing?* Now that was something I never thought I'd see. "My name's Jay." The words slipped out, and Adam's eyebrows rose. Robbie rested a heavy hand on my shoulder and squeezed.

"I'm probably about to make the biggest mistake of my life, but Adam is going to take care of you. Take some of your frustration out on the treadmill. It will help. I promise."

It wasn't a bad idea. Losing myself in some exercise would be therapeutic. "I don't have anything to wear."

"I can fix you up with some staff kit. No problem," Adam said.

I went to follow him and glanced back at Robbie, who seemed a little edgy. He wouldn't meet my eyes, but Adam got the benefit of his most intimidating glare's full force.

"No touching."

Adam smirked and led me away. The locker room was immaculate, not a stray towel or sweaty sock in sight.

"You could eat your lunch off this floor." I gazed around in amazement. Adam chuckled as he pulled sealed bags from a cupboard.

"Robbie would have my hide if it wasn't pristine."

"Is he the manager, then?" I really hadn't thought about Robbie as anything other than a bouncer.

Adam stared at me, his eyes glinting with amusement. "You really don't know, do you?"

"Know what?"

"Robbie isn't the manager, Jay. He's the owner — and not just of this place. He owns several buildings around the city. He has some other…side-lines too."

My jaw dropped and Adam laughed. "What did you think he did? You've seen his house, haven't you?"

"I don't know what I thought. Rich family, maybe? To me, he's a nightclub bouncer and he's saved my arse on several occasions."

"Mm-m." Adam sounded like he was about to choke. "He certainly thinks your arse is worth preserving. I probably shouldn't be telling you this, but Robbie took the job at Spikes as a favor to a friend who needed undercover work done beneath the radar. It was only supposed to last a few weeks, then you turned up. Robbie took one look at you and was smitten. He stayed in the job to watch over you."

I was stunned. He'd never said a word — or maybe I'd been so obsessed with my own problems that I hadn't taken the time to notice. I recalled all the times he'd been there when punters started getting rough, when he'd slipped me a bottle of cold water on busy nights, his solid presence behind me during lockdowns. I put my head in my hands. "I'm so fucking stupid. But, wait…undercover work?"

Adam tossed a T-shirt and shorts in my direction. "He's an ex-cop—military police, in fact. Here. Put these on and we can sweat the self-pity out of you. What shoe size are you?" He found a pair of his trainers that I could use then sat on the bench next to me. "Don't feel too bad. Robbie isn't the most effusive when it comes to sharing confidences. It's taken me months to wheedle this information out of him. He takes 'strong silent type' to a whole new level."

I changed quickly, trying to ignore Adam's eyes on my body. He was not subtle when it came to eyeing me up.

"Very nice. Robbie must have the patience of a saint."

I rolled my eyes at him, and he laughed. "Don't worry. My boyfriend is out there on the judo mat. He's a third dan and very possessive. Not only that, but Robbie would break me in half if I laid a finger on you."

"So what is this place? It's not a normal gym."

"No. Membership here is by invitation only and costs a fortune. The staff are well paid, but we're on call twenty-four hours a day and there is a strict code of discipline. We sign a contract that means we can't drink, smoke or take any kind of drugs. Prescriptions have to be approved. We also have to sign non-disclosure agreements. We're not allowed to talk about the members outside this building."

"Why the secrecy?"

"The clients come here for privacy. We have rock stars, powerful businessmen, politicians… They drop their jobs at the door and do as they're told in here. We offer Olympic-standard training in most martial arts and conditioning training regimes. It's not glamorous, but we guarantee discretion. For some of them, this is the only place they get some peace."

"Robbie must have a lot of interesting friends." I was beginning to understand a bit more about Robbie's life and was humbled that he had been protecting me for so long. I wondered if he realized how much I liked him.

Adam and I walked out into the gym and I took a second look at some of the men training. A couple were familiar, but out of context I couldn't be sure who they were, and I didn't want to stare like a star-struck adolescent. I couldn't see Robbie anywhere. Adam took me over to the treadmill and fastened the quick-stop wire to my waistband.

"You'll have no control over the speed of the machine once we get going, I set everything remotely. If you move too far back on the track because you can't keep up, this will pull off and shut the machine down gradually. That avoids the problem of you landing on your arse in a heap and embarrassing me."

"Embarrassing *you*? I'll be the one sprawled on the floor!"

"It's my job to understand your limits and push you just hard enough. You fall off, and it's my fault. Okay, we'll warm you up with a quick walking pace."

Over the next hour, Adam demonstrated my inadequacies. We moved from the treadmill to free weights then stretching. I think I lost about twenty pounds in sweat, but it felt good. While I lay flat on my back on the mats, chest heaving, my mind was clearer than it had since I'd left home.

Adam held out a hand and hauled me to my feet. "You did really well. I hope you become a regular. I'll enjoy whipping you into shape."

I'd been so focused on not making a complete idiot of myself that I hadn't noticed Robbie working out in the dojo area of the club. He came over and thanked Adam for his time.

"No problem, Boss. Bring him back four or five times a week and, in a few months, I might be able to do something with him."

I groaned pitifully, but Robbie nodded in agreement and I knew there was a conspiracy at work. I left them talking and headed for the locker room. There was a pile of fluffy towels inside the door, so I stripped off my sweat-soaked clothes, grabbed one then stepped into the showers. It was one big tiled area with water sprays at head and waist level. The jets were hot and powerful, perfect for my tired muscles. Containers on the walls dispensed lemon-scented body wash, and I spent a blissful five minutes soaping myself down.

I don't know how long Robbie had been watching me, but when I turned around, he was there with a towel wrapped around his waist that was tented at the front. Though his stance was relaxed, his expression was tense. I took in his powerful arms and broad chest, every muscle defined beneath the tattoos and coating of dark hair. I swallowed hard. Just looking at him was making my cock swell and I didn't have the benefit of a concealing towel.

A knowing smile quirked Robbie's lips. He held my eyes and dropped the towel. I couldn't stop my gasp. I didn't think in inches. All my lust-crazed brain could manage was a range of words for 'big'. His cock was thick, huge, the root buried in curling dark hair. My lips parted and I sank to my knees in the spray, praying he would accept my silent invitation.

"You're so pretty, Jay." Robbie's voice rumbled like thunder as he took a couple of strides toward me. "I don't want you doing this out of some sense of obligation." His dick swayed enticingly in front of my eyes, and I moaned in frustration, dropping a hand to my own painful erection. "No. No touching." I glanced up at him, startled. His gentle tone had changed to a commanding one and it sent a thrill through my body. "Hands behind your back so I know you're not cheating."

I clasped my wet hands together as he gripped my hair and pulled me toward him. That first sweet taste was burned into my memory the instant my tongue brushed across his tip. I felt like a starving man, my appetite only to be sated by taking my fill of him. But Robbie was totally in control. He rationed my pleasure with his iron grip on my hair, and I was forced to be content with quick licks and a squeeze of my lips.

I glanced up at him with pleading eyes until he relented, allowing me to edge closer. There was no way my mouth and throat could take him all, but I did my heroic best. I must have been doing something right, because Robbie's massive thighs were rigid, like from the effort of standing still. He made no noise as I worked my tongue up and down his length, pressing my teeth gently into his sensitive flesh. I can't describe how good he tasted, how wonderful it was to have that amazing girth filling my mouth.

He yanked my head away from him. "Close!"

I sacrificed some strands of hair and took him as deeply as I could. He came hard into my throat and I concentrated on swallowing, almost running out of breath by the time he had finished.

I barely had time to recover before he pulled me to my feet and shoved me back against the tiles, one hand circling my dick. What he did with that hand sent me to heaven. He was rough then gentle, quick then tortuously slow, and all the while he was crushing my lips into submission. I screamed my release, not caring who heard.

Robbie held me up, stroking my arse. My legs were jelly, and my insides were no better. He chuckled, turned the water off then passed me a towel.

"Get dressed. You have to work tonight."

So few words needed to turn a dream into a nightmare.

* * * *

Spikes was busier than ever that night. Robbie guarded the door to the staff room while I squeezed myself into leather and latex. I was more aware than ever of how tight the clothes were as Robbie's dark eyes roamed the length of my body.

"Don't look at me like that."

He grinned then disappeared into the club.

The hours passed slowly as I heaved drinks between crowded tables. Midnight came and went, and my shirt went with it. I felt more self-conscious than usual as the punters stripped the rest of my clothes with their eyes.

Every now and again I would spot Robbie making sure I was okay. There had been no sign of Urquhart's henchman, but it was crowded and I could have missed him. At closing time, Robbie indicated he would wait outside in the alley while I changed. I traded leather trousers for faded jeans and pulled on a navy T-shirt and sweater. I left by the fire exit but couldn't see Robbie. There was no one around and it took a while for my eyes to adjust to the darkness. The streetlamp in front of the club had been smashed yet again and I could see shards of orange glass glinting on the pavement. I walked down the alley a little way.

"Robbie, where are you?" My unease faded when he appeared, silhouetted against the brighter light at the end of the alley. It wasn't until he got quite close to me that I realized he was being followed and that the man pressed close behind him had a gun shoved against his head. There was blood running down Robbie's face from a cut above his eye. They stopped and two more men appeared at the end of the alley, blocking any escape route. One of them stepped forward.

"If you want your friend to survive the night, you'll come with us, Jay. It's you we want, and I would like to avoid collateral damage."

"Don't do it, Jay." Robbie growled and another blow connected with his jaw.

"Stop it." I took a shaky step toward them. "Leave him alone. I'll come with you." I held up my hands, choking back a sob. One of the goons clouted Robbie with the gun and he crumpled to the ground. I tried to go to him but two men grasped my arms.

"He has a hard head. He'll be fine." A pair of handcuffs snapped tightly around my wrists and I was shoved toward a parked limousine. "You've caused us a great deal of trouble."

The street was deserted and there were no witnesses to see me being pushed into the back of the car. There was a man on either side of me and my arms were crushed painfully behind my back. A gag was shoved into my mouth and tied tightly behind my head.

"Let's go. This little shit has to answer to the boss."

The car pulled away, and there was nothing I could do about it.

Chapter Three

The murky light of a new dawn crept over the concrete horizon as the limousine pulled down a quiet Westminster side street. It ended at the muddy water of the Thames and I wondered briefly what a property in this street must cost. Andrew Urquhart either came from money or he was supplementing his politician's income with some shady dealings. Reaching the last house in the row, the car turned in to a drive that sloped sharply downward to a garage door. The parking space beneath the house was easily big enough to store three cars.

I shivered in the dank atmosphere as I was pulled from the back of the car. Still handcuffed and gagged, I was manhandled through a door then up a set of concrete steps. A second door at the top opened into a large kitchen filled with the kind of high-end catering equipment found in a restaurant. There was a narrow, barred window on one wall, just below ceiling height, which told me we were still at basement level.

I glanced around, searching for anything that might have potential as a weapon, but there were no conveniently placed knife blocks, weighted pans or crockery that might have inflicted damage on the two apes holding my arms. It was academic, anyway. With my hands cuffed behind me, I didn't stand a chance.

In one corner of the room was a large dog cage, containing nothing but a ragged blanket. It must have housed a sizeable dog and I wondered where it was. The attention of an aggressive German shepherd was not something I craved. Five minutes later I was wishing there *was* a pet pooch around, because it may have objected to me being shoved into its sleeping accommodation. I struggled and fought, but they forced me to crawl into the cage and they padlocked the door. There was just enough room to sit—or lie down if I bent my legs—but that was it. The two goons had a good laugh, prodding at me through the bars with the end of a rolling pin, of all things. It hurt and I couldn't get away, so I lay on my side, facing away from them so they couldn't see the pain or humiliation that would surely show on my face.

Eventually they got bored and sat talking at the kitchen table. They discussed dog racing and some girl they both fancied, but nothing of importance. Aching and cramped, I tried not to think about what might happen next and drifted into an uncomfortable doze.

There was one of those old-fashioned school clocks on the wall that ticked loudly enough to ensure that I was constantly reminded of its presence. So when the door opened and a new face arrived, I knew it was a little after ten in the morning. I opened my eyes just a crack and examined the new arrival through my lashes. My two watchmen stood and their faces took on a veneer of respect, so I guessed this man had to be someone important. He was slim and expensively dressed in a tailored three-piece suit and clean-shaven, his light brown hair receding at the temples. I guessed he must be in his early forties or thereabouts, but his unlined skin made it difficult to tell. His eyes made the biggest impression. Small, dark and set too close together, they were cold and emotionless. He stared at me, showing no surprise that there was a boy imprisoned in the kitchen. When he spoke, his voice was thin and reedy but authoritative.

"He's awake. You know what to do. Make sure he is properly prepared or you'll answer to me." He turned on a well-shod heel then left. As soon as the door had closed, various gestures were made in its direction and none of them were polite.

"Fucking cocksucker. Who made him God?"

"It's whose cock he's sucking that's important. Remember that."

There was a grunt and a shrug. "Better him than me. I'd lay money that Urquhart's dick is as poisonous as his heart."

His companion snorted agreement. "Then it's a bloody good job he doesn't fancy either of us!" He leaned over my cage and spat through the bars. "You however, are a different matter. I'm sure he's going to have a lot of fun with a pretty little thing like you."

The lid of the dog cage lifted off, so they didn't drag me out through the same small doorway I'd gone in. After several hours bent into a fetal position with my arms pulled behind me, I could barely force my tortured limbs to move. The gag came off and took some of my skin with it. I hadn't realized that numb lips was a recognized condition, but I think I could have kissed Godzilla at that point and not felt a thing.

The handcuffs were removed and I resisted the temptation to massage my bruised flesh. I'd be damned if I was going to let these bastards know how much I was hurting. I looked from one goon to the other. "Well? What now? I suppose you two beat the crap out of me?"

I think a beating might have been a more enjoyable option. I was escorted up two flights of stairs and along a corridor where I literally sank into the deep pile carpet. Halfway along, I was stopped while a door was opened to reveal a palatial bathroom. Every wall was mirrored and I was confronted by my own image reflected back at me over and over. The man I saw looked exhausted, dirty and bruised, but the spark of defiance reflected in my eyes remained. My treatment so far — and what had been done to Robbie — served to make me even more determined not to give in to my fear.

"Okay, Jay, you can call me Steve, and my friend here is Chas. We have to get you ready for a meeting with Mr. Urquhart and he has made some very particular specifications regarding your appearance. You can make this as easy or as difficult as you like. The end result will be the same."

I didn't understand what was going on. I was standing in a bathroom with two blokes who could have been part of an experiment to identify the missing link, and they didn't appear to be going anywhere.

"Strip." Chas was a lot less conversational than his mate.

I backed up against the sink and shook my head.

"That wasn't a suggestion, Jay. Let me make this nice and plain. You can undress yourself and take a shower, or Chas here will hold you down while I tear your fucking clothes off. Now, what's it to be?"

Chas took one menacing step toward me, and I decided that dignity was no longer an essential part of my life. I grappled with buttons and zips, but soon I was standing there in my skimpy briefs.

Steve gave an exaggerated sigh. "Don't be shy, Jay. I'm sure you don't normally shower in your underwear."

I wasn't quick enough for Chas, who growled then ripped my underwear off before propelling me into the double-width cubicle. I covered myself with my hands as he leaned past me to turn on the powerful spray.

"There's soap, shampoo and a razor in there. Use them. You've got five minutes."

"You want me to shave in the shower?" Sometimes I could be remarkably slow on the uptake but, in my defense, it had been a stressful night.

Steve smirked unpleasantly. "You can shave your face afterward. Everything else you do in there... Be careful not to cut yourself."

"You've got to be fucking joking!"

"I can always ask Chas to give you a hand."

"No! No. I'll do it."

Thank God for steam. At least that spared me the humiliation of the two of them watching as I struggled to shave myself. For once I was grateful that I had so little body hair. It all took time and I was still rinsing when Steve pushed the cubicle door open. I climbed out, dripping and shivering, hoping there would be a towel to hand, but apparently I had to pass inspection first. Chas checked everywhere — and I mean everywhere. He grunted and threw me a small towel that just about fit around my waist. There was a fresh disposable razor next to the sink and a small can of shaving foam. I took the hint and lathered my face before scraping away the light layer of stubble.

"Dry your hair."

The only available towel was the one around my waist. I felt the prick of tears and fought down my simmering emotions.

When my hair was just damp, the towel was taken away. Chas gripped my arm and pulled me down the corridor to another room. I didn't resist. The idea of being caught stark naked in the corridor by some unsuspecting maid was a good motivator. The new room contained a bed and a chest of drawers but little else. It still reeked of money, with heavy, ornate drapes at the window and a Persian rug over the cream carpet. A sharp slap across my bare arse brought me back to reality.

"Those are for you. Get dressed." Chas gestured at some clothes laid out on the bed.

There wasn't much—a pair of boxer briefs made from black fishnet and a pair of low-rise black jeans made from the softest denim I'd ever felt. There was no shirt and no footwear. I pulled the underwear on and might as well have gone commando. I wondered what Robbie would have thought of them and swallowed. I wouldn't mind him seeing me in them, but anyone else? *No way.*

The trousers were a perfect fit, tight around my arse and thighs but not constricting. They sat low, below the line of my hipbone, and my cheeks burned as I turned in to Steve's evil smirk.

"Well, don't you look a picture?" He threw me a comb. "Sort your hair out, Goldilocks." I scowled and raked it through my tangled locks. "Better. Chas, do the honors, please."

I think it was the first time I'd seen Chas smile, and it wasn't a pleasant sight. He pulled handcuffs from his pocket and dangled them from one finger. I shivered and had to stop myself from begging him not to put them on. He twisted my arms behind my back and I winced as the cold metal snapped shut around my bruised wrists.

"Time to meet the boss."

I had to wonder about all this meticulous preparation. If Urquhart wanted me dead, he'd had plenty of opportunity. I didn't have much time to consider his motivation, however, as I was pushed and prodded along another anonymous corridor and up yet another flight of stairs. I'm not too proud to admit that I was scared, but my fear was tempered by a healthy dose of irritation.

The house was eerily quiet. We were in central London and I would have expected to be able to hear traffic, even if it was muted, but this place cut out the world completely. Our procession came to a halt outside a pair of double doors at the end of a hall. Chas tightened his iron grip on my bicep. I tested his mood and tried to pull away.

"Keep still, you fucker." His hand connected with the back of my head but then he stroked my hair back into place. So, Urquhart wouldn't like it if I wasn't presented perfectly. My stomach knotted. If someone like Chas was so careful around him, what kind of monster was he?

Steve disappeared through the doors while Chas and I stood in silence. My legs shook, and had there been any hair left on my body, I'm pretty sure it would have been standing on end. When the door opened, I jumped like a startled rabbit.

Steve pulled the door wide and gestured for us to come in. Chas' shove propelled me into a vast study, lined with shelves of leather-bound books. Behind a mahogany desk, Andrew Urquhart reclined in a leather chair, his hands behind his head, smiling. He wore a white button-down shirt and striped blue tie.

There was something about him that made me think of a snake — cold, emotionless. Even his unpleasant smile didn't reach his eyes. The way I was dressed made me feel vulnerable and I guessed that this ritual of preparation had been designed to ensure that I was off balance.

A flick of manicured fingers sent Chas and Steve away, the door whispering closed behind them. I wished they had stayed. At least their controlled aggression was recognizable for what it was. Urquhart seemed a lot more dangerous and unpredictable.

"Hello, Jay. It's nice to see you again." When he spoke, Urquhart's voice was sibilant. I half expected to see a forked tongue flicker from between his lips. He stood and, behind my back, I clenched my hands into fists. "I've been looking forward to this moment for some time."

I didn't reply but held his narrow gaze. Urquhart leaned against the edge of his desk and looked at me with thoughtful contemplation. "I've had quite a few sleepless nights to consider what to do with you. Now that you are finally here… I may have to rethink a little." He picked up a letter opener and began to play with it, twisting the blade between his pale fingers. *Too pale.* I realized that he was wearing latex gloves. "I had forgotten how attractive you are." My eyes followed the silver blade as he took two steps toward me. I took one back. "Keep still. There's nowhere for you to run. Behave yourself and you might stay in one piece a little longer."

His words didn't give me much hope for my life expectancy, but buying time seemed like a good idea, so I stood still as he approached and circled behind me.

I flinched when the cold tip of the knife grazed my bare shoulder then ran down my arm. A thin line of blood appeared on my skin, proving just how sharp the blade was. Urquhart brushed the back of my neck with gloved fingers then trailed them down my spine to rest lightly on my hip. He was so close behind me that I could feel the warmth of his breath.

"I wonder what you think I should do with someone who has caused me as much trouble as you have. How do you think you should repay the not-insignificant cost of tracking you down?"

"I've already paid a high enough price for your actions, murderer." My mouth was dry and my voice cracked as I summoned the courage to speak. My words didn't stop the passage of his hand across my chest, but he pinched each nipple viciously in response and I gasped at the sudden pain.

"Such an emotive word. But then you do wear your heart on your sleeve, don't you, Jay? The moment you saw my ring that night, what you knew was written all over your face."

His hands were wandering now, touching and stroking, twisting my nipples until they burned. When he hit me, it came as a complete shock. I hadn't seen his hand rise, hadn't braced myself for the impact, so when his fist connected with my face, I fell , crashing into a bookcase. I stayed upright, just. The taste of my own blood did nothing for my composure and it wasn't the most sensible idea to retaliate, but I did. I lowered my head and ran at him. He was still recovering from throwing the punch and I was rewarded with a satisfying grunt as the air whooshed from his lungs. It didn't stop him from getting in another blow and this time I lost my balance, landing awkwardly on my side, unable to protect myself from the fall. My shoulder took most of the impact and something tore. I yelled in pain.

Urquhart was at his desk, pulling something from a drawer. Before I could react, he punctured my flesh and emptied a syringe into my vein. He twisted his hand into my hair and pulled me to my knees, yanking my head back.

"You've caused me enough aggravation, you little fuck, but dying quick's too easy for you." Spittle flecked my cheek and I tried to pull away, but Urquhart was prepared this time. His face was mottled red, his eyes bright with anger, all his calm control gone. "The drug in your system will work quickly. You'll be aware of everything I do to you but you'll be incapable of resisting. Can you feel it yet? Like lead in your limbs?" He hissed his vitriol into my ear, digging his nails into my damaged shoulder.

To my horror, heaviness spread through my body. Movement became impossible. Urquhart pushed me down onto the floor and stood over me, grinning.

"You just lie there and relax."

My pounding head made me worry about my earlier injury but this faded into insignificance compared to my throbbing shoulder and the pain of my bound arms crushed beneath me. The sting of my cut lip and ache of my bruised face were all too real, but I could move little more than my eyes. It was terrifying.

When Urquhart knelt across me and brushed the tips of his gloved fingers across my stomach, my horror must have shown expression, because his smile spoke of intense satisfaction. He loosened his tie, pulled it off then rolled up his shirtsleeves until they were at the same point above his elbows. His movements were precise, meticulous. He paused to brush away an imaginary piece of lint then met my eyes with a gaze that projected pure evil.

Every single muscle I possessed strained to move. My body was trying to meet its obligations for fight or flight, but the drug in my system crushed those instincts mercilessly. Inside I screamed as Urquhart slid cold fingers beneath my waistband before flicking open the stud.

"I had these jeans ordered especially for you. You'll look even better without them."

Denim slid down my thighs. I couldn't raise my head, but I didn't have to see to know that Urquhart was staring at my dick through black fishnet. He licked his lips. My heart was pounding and my breath came in short, shallow gasps. He hadn't touched me and I was already heading toward panic. *Fuck, what a wuss!* Okay, I was hurting, but pain meant I was alive. My position wasn't enjoyable, but I'd faced degradation at Spikes every night for months and survived. I could live through whatever Urquhart had planned.

When he touched me, my mind shifted into reverse and I did a mental U-turn that any politician would have been proud of. If I'd been physically able, I would have convulsed. Bile rose in my throat and hot tears slipped down my face. He ran his finger the length of my inner thigh. My muscles twitched.

"So smooth…" He was talking to himself while his fingers drifted, then he started to touch the net of those stupid bloody shorts. "So much prettier shaved…." He laid his open palm across my limp cock then squeezed. "Small but perfectly formed…"

Oh, for fuck's sake. Small? Now he was adding insult to injury. It was just what I needed to reignite the spark of defiance within me. I strained against the paralysis and was rewarded as my head lifted a little.

I don't know if it was the drugs or my disgust, but my cock failed to respond to Urquhart's increasingly urgent manipulation. He growled his frustration and tore the shorts down to my knees to get better access. He pushed my legs farther apart and began to grope beneath me, pushing his fingers toward my vulnerable entrance. The first digit breached me and my neck chorded with the strain of an unvoiced scream. He was forcing his fat finger, wrapped in rubber and without any lubrication, into my channel and it was agonizing.

He laughed and withdrew before rolling me onto my front. The skimpy shorts were ripped completely away, and he pulled my arse cheeks apart and stabbed his finger into me again. My wrists pushed hard against restraining metal and tears flooded my face, dampening the carpet beneath my cheek as he tore into my body with a second finger, then a third. Then his weight was gone and I forced my head around to see what he was doing. He had another syringe in his hand, saw me watching and squirted a little of the liquid into the air.

"When I'm done fucking you, they'll find your body dumped in some dingy alley with the rubbish, and you'll be just another junkie whore who turned his last trick. I'll comfort your grieving family at your funeral and sympathize with your father over his errant son. I look good in black."

He sank the needle into my flesh and my vision blurred. Strangely, the last thing I heard as Urquhart knelt across me was the sound of splintering wood. Then everything went dark.

* * * *

Another fucking hospital. Unbelievable. I knew before I opened my eyes where I was. I couldn't mistake the smell of industrial-strength disinfectant. As I hauled myself through the white fog of semi-consciousness, I was surprised to be waking up at all. Then the pain started and I realized that being awake was not such a good place to be.

My anguished moan brought rapid footsteps to my bedside, then the warmth of something flushing my veins. A cushion of mild euphoria and pain fading to a mild ache followed.

"Better?" A green-clad nurse came into focus.

I nodded, relieved to find that I could move again.

"Okay, sweetie. Just relax while I fetch the doctor."

My field of vision expanded. This was not a normal hospital. Low lighting, subtle colors and pictures on the walls were a giveaway. The flat screen and a jug of iced water on the bedside table sealed the deal. This was a private clinic — and an expensive one.

The door to my room swooshed open. I expected a doctor, but instead saw a gorgeous man-mountain. Robbie's eyes were red-rimmed, his hair tangled. He looked like he hadn't slept in a while, but when his eyes met mine, his face cracked into a beaming smile.

"Hey, sleepyhead." He took two long paces to the edge of my bed and picked up my hand, rubbing his thumb across my palm. "How are you feeling?"

"Better, now that you're here. What the hell happened, Robbie? Where am I?"

He squeezed my hand and laid it gently back on the covers. "I can answer the second part. You're in a private clinic in London. As for the first part, that will take a little longer and I don't want to tire you out."

I started to protest but he gave me his best 'behave yourself' look and I collapsed back onto the pillows.

Whatever drugs I'd been given were making me drowsy and I felt cushioned from reality. The world was in soft focus. Even the hard planes of Robbie's body seemed less defined.

"You're so handsome..." I giggled.

Robbie smiled indulgently and tousled my hair as if I were an errant child. "I think you need to rest, Jay. Close your eyes. I'll be here when you wake up. I promise."

When I did come back to the land of the living for the second time, he was asleep in the chair next to my bed. He looked much younger in sleep, and I realized that I didn't actually know how old he was. His eyes flickered open and his forehead creased with concern.

"How do you feel? Shall I fetch the doc?"

"No. It's okay." I took a moment to test the aches in my body. My shoulder hurt the most and I could feel heavy strapping around it. My face ached and my lower lip seemed tight and swollen. What worried me more was the relentless throbbing in my arse. I lifted a shaking hand to brush the hair out of my eyes and winced at the livid bruising around my wrists. "Urquhart?"

Robbie scowled. "When the police got to you, you were alone. They made a lot of noise getting into the house and that piece of slime had time to get away. The only other person they found was Urquhart's personal assistant and he denied that Urquhart had even been there."

"He was there, Robbie. It was him that did all this—" My voice broke and I shut my eyes in despair.

"Jay"—he stroked my cheek—"look at me." I opened my eyes. "I believe you, but without proof, there's little we can do."

"How the hell can they explain away a drugged, handcuffed boy in a politician's private study?"

"An act of charity. You weren't cuffed when we found you. The story is that Urquhart's secretary saw you lying in the street, picked you up in his car and took you back to the house. He said he was in the process of calling an ambulance to get you to a hospital."

"Fuck. And what about you? His goon hit you hard."

"Not as hard as he thought. I followed the car on the bike. I still can't believe Urquhart was arrogant enough to have you taken to his own home. Fucker thinks he's untouchable, but I called in a few favors and the Met responded to an 'anonymous tip-off' that an armed robbery was in progress."

"He is untouchable, though. Isn't he? He's just proved it."

Robbie blinked. "We'll see."

"What aren't you telling me, Robbie?" But that was it. He reverted to type, and I got no more information out of him.

* * * *

Two days later I was allowed to go home. I'd spent most of those days protesting that I was fine and should be allowed to leave, but Robbie sided with the doctor and ensured I was confined to bed. The drugs had cleared my system but left me weak. I had to admit that I still felt awful, but the bruises were healing and the doc assured me — after the most humiliating exam I've ever had — that I'd suffered no permanent damage. Urquhart hadn't got past using his fingers on me, but he hadn't been gentle. I was thankful the drugs fogged my memory of the abuse.

Robbie waited while I dressed in the new clothes he had brought then escorted me from the building, one hand on the small of my back, as if he were afraid I would fall. It felt good. Robbie's powerful bike was out front, but so was a chauffeur-driven car, which he ushered me toward. He didn't give me a chance to complain, just guided me into the back seat.

"Sit. Rest. I'll be right behind you."

I gave him a salacious grin, and he rolled his eyes as he slammed the door on my implied innuendo. The car was a good decision. I doubted I would have been a safe passenger on the back of the bike, and by the time we reached home, I was nodding off. When I said 'home' I meant Robbie's house. He allowed no debate as he took me inside, stood watching with his arms folded as I undressed then tucked me into bed.

* * * *

The next two days passed in a blur, and the week that followed brought a gradual reduction in my aches and pains. I watched the news, eager for some sign that Urquhart had been arrested, but there was no mention of him. I surfed the web on Robbie's computer, looking for local constituency information, but the only story I could find referred to some obscure foreign trade exchange. In the end, Robbie changed his password and banned me from doing anything more stressful than playing solitaire, because every time I came off the machine, I'd felt depressed and a nagging fear ate into my bones.

As soon as I was well enough, Robbie made sure I took regular trips to the gym, and it did help. That bastard Adam might look as though butter wouldn't melt in his mouth, but he was a remorseless slave driver when it came to my fitness.

After a particularly nasty evening session that had left me aching and soaked with sweat, I dismounted from the pillion seat, took off my helmet and gave Robbie a world-class scowl. He stowed his gear with a slight smile then looked at me strangely. I was standing on the pavement, wearing a tight black T-shirt, leather bike trousers and boots. The T-shirt was clinging to my body from the residual heat of the leather jacket I had just shrugged off and my hair was still tousled from a combination of helmet hair and showering at the gym.

Robbie towered over me, and for a moment, just looked me up and down, then he seemed to come to a decision. "Fuck it. I don't have the patience for martyrdom, though you could challenge the morals of a saint." He picked me up and threw me over his shoulder, one hand pressed firmly against my arse to stop me from falling. I squirmed and kicked but it was no use. He shoved the front door open and took the stairs two at a time. Then I was weightless, sailing through the air to land on the enormous bed in the master bedroom.

As I shuffled as close to the safety of the headboard as I could get, Robbie stripped off his T-shirt in one smooth motion. I couldn't restrain my gasp at the sight of his dark-furred chest and the fascinating trail of hair that led downward.

"I can't take it anymore, Jay, looking at you every day and not having you. I know I don't deserve you...but I thought, after the shower the other week, that you might feel something too?"

It was a long sentence for Robbie. He seemed to take the fact that I stayed on the bed as encouragement. He kicked off his boots and yanked down his leathers. He wasn't wearing anything underneath. *Oh. My. God.* I closed my gaping mouth and met his eyes. For once I had nothing to say. Instead, I pulled off my T-shirt and gave him an anxious smile.

He bent over me, his massive erection prodding my thigh, and removed the rest of my clothes. His movements were assured and confident, mine nervous and shaky. I tried to relax against the pillows as he knelt across me but couldn't restrain the twitch as he touched me for the first time.

"Relax, Jay. I promise I won't hurt you. This only goes as far as you want it to."

He stroked my pale skin as if I were the tiniest kitten, and I responded with a purr. The blond down on my legs had grown, but I had decided to keep my groin shaved. The itch of returning hair had been unbearable. Robbie brushed the backs of his fingers across my taut stomach and followed the curve of my neck and shoulders with the pads of his thumbs. He went nowhere near my cock—or even my ultra-sensitive nipples—and I wanted to scream at him in frustration. He moved closer, brushing my inner thighs, circling the hardened nubs on my chest. Every now and again his cock would press into me, reminding me of just how big he was.

He wetted his thumbs and began to agitate my nipples. I arched and moaned over his chuckle of amusement.

"Like that, huh?"

His tongue and the gentle nipping of even white teeth replaced his thumbs. His beard scraped against my skin and I bucked in ecstasy. He kept on laving my sensitive flesh and reached between my legs to firmly grasp my throbbing dick.

"Oh! Holy crap!"

Two strokes, maybe three, and I came all over his hand, shuddering and gasping from the sheer pleasure of it.

Robbie gave me time to recover before neatly rolling onto his back and sitting me across his thighs. He grabbed a condom from the bedside table, ripped the packet open, rolled it on then reached for the lube.

"I'm big enough to hurt you, Jay. Are you sure about this?"

"I've wanted you for months, Robbie. I want you to be my first."

"Wait!" He clamped his hand across my thigh. "You're a *virgin*?"

I nodded, worried that it would put him off but not prepared to lie.

"You might want to use a lot of this!" Grinning, he handed me the lube. "Take your time." He grasped my hips but applied no pressure.

I took one of his hands and squeezed clear gel onto *his* fingers. "Stretch me?"

My dick was already hard again, but as his first finger penetrated me, it jumped to attention. It hurt a little, but Robbie was careful. I nodded my assent and a second finger joined the first to create a slow burn. Robbie cupped my arse with his other hand and I fucked myself on his fingers, slowly at first, then faster. It felt so damn good, wiping out all memories of Urquhart.

I had no idea how my body was ever going to accommodate Robbie's massive cock, but I couldn't wait any longer. I tugged his hand away and spent a few happy moments tormenting him as I slicked his cock with lube. He returned the favor by smoothing more gel around my hole and gave me an encouraging smile.

It was all down to me. I spread my legs wide and sank down until I could feel his tip nudging my entrance. He'd stretched me enough that the first inch was not too bad. I got complacent and moved a bit quicker but gasped at the pain caused by the next two. *Fuck, it hurts.* I panted, relaxed my muscles as best I could and slowly sank down on him. I couldn't move. Impaled by a red-hot poker… That was how it felt. I was so full. I opened my eyes and gazed at Robbie. He looked like he was in pain too and I realized belatedly that just lying there must be agonizing for him. My muscles wouldn't work. I tapped the huge hands around my hips and he took the hint, raising and lowering me just a little. I gasped as the movement agitated the delicate bundle of nerves inside me. Robbie growled. He lifted me farther, lowering me gently at first, then dropping me so that my arse hit his thighs with a slap. Once the pain faded to a dull throb, I could concentrate on the intense pleasure. I screamed, laughed, cried — all together, I think — but when Robbie came, he squeezed my cock and I joined him in a release that was emotional as well as physical.

Robbie softened inside me as I snuggled into his chest.

"Are you okay?" he murmured and I felt the vibrations of his deep voice and the gentle tug of his fingers in my hair.

"Mm-m," was all I could manage in response as I drifted into a deep, dreamless sleep.

* * * *

When I woke the next morning, aching and sore, I was relieved the bed next to me was empty. A naked Robbie might have been too tempting to resist and my arse needed some recuperation time. I showered, shaved, threw on some clothes then headed downstairs. There was a cryptic note on the kitchen table.

Turn on the TV. This could be the best day of your life.

I doubted that. Making love with Robbie would take some beating.

A single story dominated the morning news programs. MP Andrew Urquhart, rising star of the government, was sought in connection with a series of frauds and suspicion of diverting weapons meant for the British Army to a range of unpleasant dictators around the globe.

"Oh!" I gasped as my father appeared on the screen, voicing his suspicions and claiming to have evidence of Urquhart's crimes. I hardly heard the rest of the piece as my own photo flashed up on the screen and details of my disappearance were made public. Suspicion of kidnap, threatening behavior… The list went on and on.

I sat on the floor, shaking. *Is the nightmare really over?* The front door clicked and my heart pounded. "Robbie…" My voice trailed into silence because the person that appeared in the doorway wasn't Robbie but my dad, tears in his eyes, arms held out. I flung myself into his welcoming embrace, aware of Robbie's looming presence behind him.

The flurry of apologies and emotion gradually calmed. I sat with my hands clasped around a mug of tea and listened as my father explained how he'd had suspicions about Urquhart for some time. The dinner I had so grudgingly attended had been designed to tempt him into an indiscretion. To his shame, my father admitted that I had been the bait, hence his insistence that I was there. Of course he'd had no idea about the ring or the attack I had witnessed. The timing had just been a disastrous coincidence.

"Of course, in the end, it had worked. Urquhart was so obsessed with getting his hands on you that he began to make silly mistakes and the evidence grew. Then Robbie here came to find me…" Dad laughed at my obvious surprise. "You have a good friend here, son." He watched my face. "More than a friend?"

I nodded, my face burning.

To my utter shock, my stern father stood and shook Robbie's enormous hand. "I couldn't be more pleased. Robbie is a fine man. And he won't take any of your… Sorry. I promised myself I wouldn't scold you."

I laughed and hugged him. "Dad, I missed you yelling at me. Just be you. I want everything back to normal."

* * * *

It was almost three weeks before Urquhart surfaced with a mouthful of lame excuses that didn't prevent his arrest. I returned home to my family then moved back to Robbie's place after clearing out my apartment.

There was still the trial to face and a return to college to finish my degree. But there would be no more working at Spikes, thank God. I was going to help out at the gym so I could contribute to my keep. I wasn't comfortable relying on Robbie, even though he was happy to support me while I studied.

I sighed as he wrapped his strong arms around me and I slipped my hand into his trousers to stroke his massive cock. It was iron hard, as usual. *Fuck, the man has stamina.* He bent to kiss me, scraping his beard across my smooth face.

"Behave!"

I shook my head and carried on groping happily. The nearest soft surface was the hearthrug and I soon found myself unceremoniously stripped and dumped onto it. Robbie pushed my legs back and gave my arse a firm smack. He stripped then pulled my legs over his shoulders. I didn't know where the lube came from, but I gave thanks that Robbie was always prepared. At least he didn't need to hunt for condoms now that we had been tested and agreed to be exclusive so that we could go bare. Despite his strength, he was always gentle with me and I was usually the one begging for him to claim me with more force. He slid into me — a perfect fit. I couldn't imagine ever being satisfied by anyone else.

As his muscles flexed and he took me to heaven, I looked into his eyes and whispered, "I love you."

When he responded in kind, my heart fluttered and I knew that even though I'd kept my silence before, I'd never again have to fear a secret's hold over me while I was held in Robbie's loving embrace.

UNDER HIS PROTECTION

CHERYL DRAGON

Chapter One

"Cartel activity in Austin is up. Not just with street-level drugs, but known members have been seen. We are in contact with the DEA, but we're not sure what's going on yet. Violent crimes have been ticking up in the past week. Obviously, Narcotics has the lead, but we're just as involved. Work your cases, but also check on your local connections. Outreach helps," Lt. Ridgeway explained.

The Violent Crimes department briefings were normally duller, but Detective Matt Blackburn had only been in the unit a few months. Not that long ago, he'd been a patrol cop in uniform.

"Blackburn," Ridgeway said.

"Lieutenant," Matt replied.

"You're the most recent off patrol, so your connections are the freshest. A lot of this is happening on your old beat, so don't be afraid to go back to your old haunts and show off the suit." Ridgeway winked.

"Yes, ma'am." Matt nodded.

Some of the men bristled at working for a woman, but even Texas had to get with the times sooner or later…

Cartel trouble wasn't something that the area had issues with. Drugs, sure, but what city didn't have that problem?

"It's kind of far north for cartel activity," Matt said to his partner as the meeting broke up.

Julie shrugged. "You can't predict it. Maybe too much activity at the border… Maybe someone stole a shipment and ran north or someone escaped and made it this far. Cartels don't like to lose people, product or money. It might just be a few cartel guys and some hired staff looking to recover something."

"There's a shelter I used to keep an eye on. Mind if we roll by?" Matt asked.

"Sounds good to me. What kind of shelter?" she inquired.

"LGBTQ+ youth—some outreach programs but mainly a shelter. Teens can get themselves in trouble quicker than anyone." Matt refilled his travel mug with coffee then they headed to their vehicle.

"You got that right. Drive, since you know the area." She tossed him the keys. "Luckily the cartel probably won't mess with them. They'll be after their problem and gone. Drawing more attention only makes their lives harder."

"Sure, but some of those kids have been in gangs or sold drugs. Most have sold other things, but it's a complicated lot. I worked security for them sometimes when they had events," Matt shared.

"Any cute guys work at this shelter?" Julie teased.

"No. It's about the kids—and I'm not into kids," Matt said firmly.

"You need a life," Julie said.

He drove in the direction of the shelter. Austin traffic was crazy, as usual. "I got a promotion. That's a life."

She rolled her big blue eyes at him. "But you have no one to celebrate with. The Violent Crimes unit can be a rough place. You need something happy in your life to balance it out. Get a puppy, at least."

Matt chuckled. "Naturally, and when will I train and take out this puppy with a job so unpredictable, as well as being on call some nights?"

"Getting a boyfriend would help. Then get a couple of kids and make them do the grunt work. That takes care of things for me," Julie said.

Her hubby taught school, so he kept a regular schedule and the kids were at the same one, so childcare was managed. They were so cute, but life didn't fall into place for everyone like it had for Julie.

Matt found himself a bit jealous at times—not wanting Julie's husband, but she had a certainty about her life. She loved her work, but family came first.

"I'll try to get a life, just for you. But with a new job learning curve to manage, it might not be the best time." Matt had mastered deflecting set-ups and pushiness. He was a new detective, but plenty of other cops had tried to fix him up during his years on the force. *Next, she'll suggest the bars or gay apps.*

"You know, a cousin of mine has had a lot of luck on the apps," Julie said.

Matt smiled. "For hookups, sure. I'm not hurting in that area. I can walk into a gay bar and get a guy. It's fun, but it's not—"

"Love. Aww-w," Julie said.

"Real," Matt corrected her quickly. "It's not *real*."

"Real love. Have you thought about a little something? A rainbow pin on your lapel maybe? You are a hyper-suit masculine guy, which is you, but you're so… Half the department is still convinced you're straight," Julie said.

Matt shrugged and finally neared the block for the Engles Memorial Shelter. "Jules, not every gay guy is flamboyant. Not every lesbian is butch. I don't need to advertise."

"I know that. I didn't mean you should change yourself at all. I just don't know if you give off the right signals. You're all about the job at work," she said.

Parking the car, Matt looked at his partner. "Am I not paying enough attention to the people we deal with?"

"No, you're good with victims and suspects, even with community outreach. You talk plenty, but it's about the case or them and *their* lives," she said.

"They don't want to talk about me. We're public servants. I'm not picking up guys who commit violent crimes and I'm sure as hell not taking advantage of a victim," he said.

"You're right. And if another cop was interested in you, I'd have heard about it. So I need to find someone to set you up with," Julie threatened.

"Please don't. I'm fine. I have horrible timing and bad luck. That's all. I'm leaving it up to fate," Matt replied as he cut the engine.

"You're going to be the weird spinster uncle at my family holidays. I can see it now. Let's go, Mr. Fate," she teased.

The duo walked into the shelter and the kids turned to look.

"Blackburn got the day off?" one of the kids asked.

"Thanks for noticing, Mario. No, I'm a detective now," Matt said.

"Detective?" Minnie stuck her head out of the office. "We were wondering what happened to you." The petite woman with short, spiky purple hair wore a flowery print dress. Min ran out and gave him a hug that lifted her off her feet. "Congrats!"

"Thanks." Matt set her down. "This is Julie, my partner."

Minnie shook Julie's hand. "Hey. Happy to have the support. Want the tour—or do you have something specific to discuss?"

"Just increased trouble in the area. See any new dealers or problems?" Matt asked.

"Nothing new that I've seen, but I'll spread the word. We got our outside lights fixed, thanks to Josh, so that helps," she said.

"Is he around?" Matt tried to sound casual. The shelter was brightened by art, but the core of the building was gray and cold. Matt had done some maintenance and was glad others pitched in to keep the place safe and functioning.

"Who is Josh?" Julie asked with a raised eyebrow.

"One of our volunteers. He works at a rehab facility by day. As a certified addictions counselor, teens are his specialty, so he gives us part of his time. So sweet. Here he just uses AA methods and he even taught the kids to run meetings for when he can't be here, but it really helps. He's also kind of handy…and good-looking." Minnie smiled.

Matt had seen Josh around a lot when he'd patrolled the area. They'd exchanged glances that made Matt want more but had only traded small talk a few times when he'd helped out at the shelter. He'd thought there were sparks, but…

"You can't keep kids under eighteen. They go to the foster system, right?" Julie asked.

Minnie shared a look with Matt. "Of course… We house eighteen through the mid-twenties. We get a lot of minor teens who drop in for a meeting, a kind word or help with a parent issue, though. Josh and Matt were behind our family outreach."

"You worked with this Josh? Is he really cute?" Julie asked.

"They sort of worked in tandem. We're running on duct tape and good vibes, so we take help when and how we can get it. Josh is very attractive, but until fairly recently, he had a guy," Minnie explained.

"We never worked *together* on anything," Matt added.

"Sure you did—but not at the same time." Minnie waved a hand at him. "Josh suggested in one of their AA group-share things that, if they were underage and at risk of getting dumped into the system, they should reach out to other family members if they weren't safe at home. Maybe they could spend the summer there or even move—with parental permission, of course."

"Of course," Julie said and shot Matt a look.

Min was looking at Matt and continued. "Then a couple of the kids asked you if it was okay. You said there was no law against talking to family members and that as long as a parent agreed, no problem with staying there. Plenty of kids stay out of the system due to family connections and by just getting a parent to agree," Minnie reminded him.

"Right. It was an off-the-cuff chat," Matt said.

Julie shrugged. "The school districts might get fussy."

"Most of these kids end up doing home school online to avoid drama or harassment, though some get that at home too. But with the home-school option through the state, there are no districting problems and some of the kids are safer with an aunt or a grandparent." Minnie never slowed down. She went through the halls, flipping off lights and putting things away.

"You wouldn't happen to have Josh's card?" Julie asked.

Minnie stopped and turned. "Why? He didn't do anything wrong."

"No, but he's single," Julie said.

"And gay. Didn't I mention that? Gay…not bi or pan. *Gay*." Minnie shot Matt a look and went back to work. "Matt has his contact info. We make sure all the volunteers have each other's numbers, in case someone can't make it or needs help."

"Thanks, Min. Just please call if you see anything weird. Keep your eyes open. Be extra safe," Matt said.

"Always. Bye, and thanks for the check-in." Minnie waved over her head as she kept on going.

Julie tried to follow but Matt steered her back toward the door.

"Josh sounds hot," Julie said.

"So hot," Mario agreed.

"Mario…" Matt said sharply.

"Sorry. Your loss, man. I respect not moving on the guy when he's got a boyfriend, but grab him while he's single. Josh's boyfriend was a cheating ass anyway. You'll be a prize and treat him better." Mario went back to helping in the office.

Back in the car, Matt felt flushed. "The kids and Minnie do *not* need encouragement when it comes to matchmaking. They could make Josh really uncomfortable."

"Josh…or you?" Julie clicked her seatbelt into place.

"I've been cheated on too. I'm not going after a guy with a boyfriend," Matt said firmly.

Julie smiled big and patted Matt's arm. "Good. Cheating is bad for any relationship. But he's not taken any longer, so that problem is solved. Obviously, Minnie and Mario think you two might make a good couple."

"Or they want something new and juicy to talk about," Matt replied.

"You think you're juicy?" She laughed.

Matt shook his head. "We're done with this. Let's go catch some bad guys."

"What's his last name?" Julie asked.

"Why?" Matt stalled by answering her question with a question.

She cocked her head to one side. "I'm looking him up. You know his last name. Don't pretend that you don't."

Matt pressed his lips together. Josh was hot, smart and kind, with sandy brown hair, blue eyes and he was tall. He wore cowboy boots with suits or jeans — anything Matt had ever seen him in included boots. No hat or big belt buckle, just the boots. He was lean but muscled enough to be handy and help around the shelter.

Julie snapped her fingers. "Hey, get off your man-filled fantasy island and tell me his last name."

"Braidshaw. He doesn't have a record." Matt pulled out into traffic and cruised the area.

"I'm looking him up on social media, not doing a background check. Oh, he's hot. Yes, you need to ask him out."

Matt shook his head. "We don't know each other *that* well. You're basing this all off his looks, and I'm not wanting a hookup. Imagine if we screwed around and it didn't work, then we're weird at the shelter. The kids lose out."

"You're both adults Plus, there's Minnie's feedback. She knows you both as people, not just hot bodies in the night. You have excellent instincts and are a wonderful judge of character. Min must be too, to run a shelter. This Josh is a good guy. He cares about things and people like you do. You're attracted to him. At least ask him out on a date."

Matt sighed. "If I promise to ask him out the next time I see him, will you drop it and not embarrass me if you happen to meet him?"

Julie looked at her phone. "Yes, but I am going to follow him on Insta and maybe run him through the work computer."

There was no stopping her, but the odds were good that Josh would never find out about it anyway. By the time Matt ran into him, Josh would probably have a new boyfriend. Guys like that didn't stay single for long.

* * * *

As always, Josh closed the meeting with the serenity prayer. Minnie seemed to be loitering in the hall, but he wasn't going to rush the wrap-up. The kids needed to know that they mattered. If it was an emergency, Minnie would have no problem busting in on things.

"Good meeting, everyone. Don't forget to sign for one-on-one chats if you need it. I'll be here Sunday afternoon. And the beef stew should be nice and warm. Eat before you leave," Josh said.

The group put the chairs back in order in the all-purpose room then headed for the kitchen.

Min smiled. "You don't always have to feed them."

Josh shrugged. "Is your food budget overflowing?"

She laughed. "I'm a vegetarian, but I'll eat around the meat."

"Veggie in Texas? Cows are delicious," Mario teased.

"Hey, Mario, a minute," Josh said.

Mario had been clean for a year and taken a job in the office. He was half resident and half employee. He was studying for his GED as well. Minnie had nearly adopted him, but he was nineteen, so he didn't need a guardian.

"Yeah, boss." Mario turned.

"Don't call me 'boss'. Have you seen Victor?" Josh asked.

"Not today." Mario shrugged.

"What do you mean? He's always at a meeting. He just up and left?" Josh frowned.

"Stuff happens. Maybe he got a fam call to come home? Maybe he relapsed. We're not supposed to go searching," Mario reminded Josh.

"Right, good call. But if you hear something…" Josh said.

Mario nodded. "Sure. I know he got a phone call and split overnight. His stuff is gone, but that's all. I'll text you if he turns up or I hear something."

"Thanks." Josh smiled.

Maybe it was nothing, but the residents and drop-ins kept secrets from the staff and volunteers. Josh hoped Mario knew more and might flush Victor out if Victor knew some adults actually cared.

Minnie waved Josh over. "Hey, so our favorite police officer resurfaced."

"Matt? Long vacation or something?" Josh filled out his volunteer forms and checked off the kids who'd attended, for their records.

"No, he's a detective now. His promotion explains the absence. I know you were missing him. He looked sharp in that suit." Minnie smiled.

"Good for him." Josh refused to take the bait. "Glad it's nothing bad. Policework can be stressful. Plenty of them turn to substances."

"Matt is strong. He and his police partner, Julie, had a warning. Increased drug activity blah-blah-blah. Be careful. But your name came up," Minnie said.

"Min..." Josh began.

"Wait—" She cut him off. "You're single. It's been at least six months since you've even talked to that evil ex or gotten a text from him. You need to move on."

"With Matt?" Josh shook his head.

"Why not? You're attracted to him. I've caught you staring. He's hot *and* nice." Minnie folded her arms.

"You're sure he's gay?" Josh asked.

"Julie was trying to find a guy for him. I get it. The uniform sort of removes signals, but he looked nice in his suit. He's still uber masculine, but that's not a bad thing. He has always taken an interest in the shelter," Minnie pointed out.

"He was a cop with an area to patrol. That was just his job." Josh didn't want to put himself out there again. He was fine on his own, but his past taste in men had proven questionable. "Let me manage my own personal life?"

"Fine. I'm just sharing the latest news and events with you. Matt is always on the job when we see him, so he has to be professional. You're a volunteer here, so you have more flexibility," she reminded him.

"Meaning?" Josh asked.

"You could ask him out. Maybe he's afraid if he did it on duty, it'd be considered inappropriate. He's an old-fashioned, by-the-book sort of guy," Minnie said.

"Or he's closeted at work. Maybe his partner is the only one who knows?" Josh grabbed his messenger bag and signed out. "See you on the weekend."

"Fine… Be that way. Die alone and old. Be safe," she called.

Josh hopped in his old pick-up and headed home slowly. The kids hung out on the street in this part of town. He'd only made it a block when he spotted Victor fighting with some other guys in an alley.

Pulling over, Josh jumped out of the truck and shouted, "Hey! What's going on?"

Josh pulled out his phone and snapped a picture as he tried to also hit the emergency call button to get nine-one-one. His hands shook too much and he dropped his phone.

One of the kids pulled a gun and fired. The bullet whizzed by Josh and he ducked. Another car turned up the street and the headlights made it hard for Josh to see.

Josh paused and tried to pick up his phone, but it was too dark. Finally, he started to backtrack to his car for safety, but he heard tires peeling out and getting closer. The car clipped him, sending him sprawling to the asphalt—then everything went black.

Chapter Two

Matt walked into the ER after inspecting the scene. Julie would cover that end for now. She'd insisted he take the interview. Matt should've probably excused himself from the case because he knew Josh through the shelter, but he felt more obligated to protect him.

Walking into room four, he flashed a badge and no one argued. Josh had his eyes closed. He was shirtless and his jeans looked torn and bloody. Keeping his professional hat on, Matt tried not to gawk at the piercing through one of Josh's nipples. It wasn't what Matt had imagined Josh would have but it was very hot. That lean swimmer's body had abs for days, but Matt could enjoy that memory later.

"How is he?" Matt asked the nurse.

Josh opened his eyes and stared into Matt's. Matt tried to give a reassuring smile. They'd never met in a normal way. There were always teens around…or professionals. Now they were in an ER.

"How's Victor? Did you find him?" Josh tried to sit up but winced.

"Please, sir. You need to lie still." The nurse gently guided Josh back to the bed.

The doc nodded to Matt and they stepped out of the room. All Matt wanted to do was comfort Josh and protect him, but he needed the info — not to climb into that bed and cuddle him or play with the nipple ring.

Matt shook his head. He wasn't a cuddler. This was work. But he still swore silently to himself that whoever had done this would pay for it.

"X-rays show hairline fractures of two ribs. We'll tape them, but he doesn't need surgery. There are a few cuts that need stitches, but mostly there's just blunt force trauma from a car. We did a scan but there's no internal bleeding. There are bruises, road rash on his arm and a possible slight concussion, but nothing to worry about. We'll stitch him up, give him some pain meds and I can release him in a few hours," the doc said.

"Good, thanks. I need to speak to him," Matt said.

"Do we need security to stand by?" the nurse asked as she left.

"No, he's a victim." Matt walked back in. "Josh, can you answer some questions for me?"

"I guess. Is Victor okay? Minnie?" Josh asked.

Matt smiled. "Minnie is fine. She's worried about you. The kids are shaken up, but this happened a block or so away from the shelter. You were driving home?" Matt asked.

Josh nodded. "You do look good in that suit. Minnie said you got promoted or something. Congrats. Not that I don't love a man in uniform, but you look more comfortable like that."

"Thanks. The doc said you might have a slight concussion but to just relax. You're safe now. Can you focus on the incident? Tell me what happened." Matt pulled a chair up and sat close to Josh.

"Victor is a newer kid—a good kid who wants to be clean. He wasn't at the meeting tonight, which was weird. Mario didn't know why. Victor got a call and booked. Maybe he owed someone money from his drug days, or maybe his family found him. He said his grandfather ran the family and gay got you beaten until you straightened out. Poor kid. Kid... I mean, he was eighteen, maybe nineteen, so he could stay at the shelter." Josh tried to sit up again.

Matt put a hand on Josh's shoulder and it seemed to ease his stress, but the tension shifted to something different. Roaming hands were not appropriate in the ER. Josh leaned back and Matt let go.

"Sorry." Josh cleared his throat. "I shouldn't take it personally, but I hate losing a kid—any of them."

"I know. I get it. We'll do everything we can to find him. Start from the beginning and tell me what happened to you." Matt patted Josh's arm.

Josh sighed and recounted the story. There were some gaps when the light blinded him and when he got hit by the car.

"Does the shelter have a picture of Victor that we can get out there?" Matt asked.

"They should. I also took a pic of the group on my phone but I can't find it." Josh started to sit up again and patted his pants.

"Relax, Josh. The nurses would've taken everything out of your pockets." Matt found a small bag of personal items. "Lip balm, a couple of dollars and change, but no phone."

"I must've dropped it. *Shit*. No car keys? My wallet?" Josh asked.

"My partner is at the scene. We'll see what she can find. Okay?" Matt tried to sound reassuring but that wasn't good. No one else had been found there. If Victor was the victim, the bad guys had either taken him and could have killed and dumped him.

Taking Josh's wallet and keys might've been deliberate. Josh could ID them. He was the witness.

Why didn't they take Josh or kill him? Maybe they thought he was dead at the scene and took the stuff for the money? Matt ran down the options, but bottom line, Josh was in danger of being hunted down to make sure he stayed silent.

"Thanks. Losing your wallet is such a pain, with credit cards and the DMV." Josh yawned.

"Could you identify those men who were with Victor if you saw them again?" Matt asked.

"I think so—at least two of them. They shot at me," Josh admitted. "Missed, but I heard the bullets go by."

Matt grabbed Josh's hand. "You know you shouldn't have gotten out of the car, right? Call the cops. Don't be a hero."

"Thanks, Mom." Josh squeezed Matt's hand. "I thought maybe Victor backslid and was just buying drugs. Then I saw their faces and they were too mature and put-together. I mean…old guys can sell drugs, but I just know the area and who runs the corners. They were too well equipped to be small-time sellers."

"Why do you say that?" Matt took his hand back to continue making notes, but he wanted more affection. It felt comfortable with Josh. The loss of contact nagged at his insides. Min and Julie had put things in his head, and now, seeing so much of Josh? It wasn't helping. But this wasn't a fundraiser at the shelter. This was life and death.

Josh shrugged and winced. "Teens usually buy from other teens. These guys were our age, at least thirty. They had nice clothes and knives, fancy guns. Maybe it was his family coming back for him? Maybe... But the car that came at me had been just sitting there and waiting. It was organized. They had backup. That was not a corner drug deal."

"No, it's not. Okay, let's give you a break. Don't give yourself a headache or more of one. Relax. It's my job to figure it out now. Tell me every detail you remember, no matter how weird, and you might remember more things. It's okay. Rest and let them stitch you up," Matt soothed his only witness.

"My phone has stuff you can use," Josh said.

The doc knocked on the door and walked in. "Do you mind, Detective?"

Matt got up. "No. I'll go check on the scene and see if we can find that phone, wallet and keys."

"Thanks," Josh said. "Wait, Detective..."

Hearing Josh call him that sent an electric need down Matt. He turned at the door. "Yeah?"

"Congrats on the promotion again." Josh smiled.

Matt nodded. "Thanks. Now rest. We'll piece it all together and find Victor. I'll be back."

* * * *

An hour later, Josh had stitches, he'd started to feel where the bruises would appear and his ribs were sore every time he moved, even a little bit. He wasn't calling his sister. She'd freak out.

"Would you like us to call anyone?" the nurse asked again.

"No, thanks," he said.

His last emergency contact had been Bill, the evil ex, the jerk who'd taken advantage of Josh's charitable nature — at least according to his sister. Bill was good at being what people wanted from him. When they'd first met, Bill had been dressed like James Bond. It had been for a Halloween costume...but a perfect one.

Like Matt was dressed tonight for work, only a tux more than suit. The spectrum of desire and types was fun for the younger kids, but Josh felt boring. His type was hyper-masculine men, plain and simple. It made Josh feel older than his pushing-thirty reality.

Looking down, Josh wanted to cover up. Being shirtless wasn't so bad, but without his phone, keys or wallet, he felt naked. He wanted Matt to come back, but what could he do? He should be out there looking for Victor.

"We can get you a warm blanket," the nurse's aide offered.

"It's fine. I just don't know what to do. Having no phone feels weird." He shrugged.

Just then, Matt walked in, and Josh felt safer. Matt's suit coat was unbuttoned and Josh glimpsed the gun on Matt's belt. *What a time to be fantasizing...* Josh needed to get his mind anywhere but where it was headed.

"Anything on Victor?" Josh asked.

"We have been looking for him. Treating it as a kidnapping. Your wallet and keys are missing, as is your vehicle. Your phone..." Matt held up a plastic bag with a smashed cell phone in it.

"Great. If they'd taken the phone, at least we could've tracked my phone's GPS. What can I do to help? Sketch artist? Give a description? Come down to the station?" Josh offered. He absently rubbed his head from the ache that wouldn't stop annoying him.

A pretty woman walked up and whispered to Matt. Matt shook his head. "We'll be right back."

Josh hoped for the best, but he had a bad feeling about Victor. The guys had been beating him up, not talking nicely. Had they found Victor's body? Josh tried to remember what they'd said to Victor.

Matt and his friend walked back in.

"Hi, I'm Julie, Matt's partner. We are going to get your apartment under surveillance. We have an APB out on your car. It's obviously been stolen. We'll get you a report for your insurance as well," she said.

"Worry about Victor. The rest, it's just stuff," Josh said.

She nodded. "I understand. But they may have used your car to throw off witnesses who saw what they were driving. Victor might be in your car. They might have picked up your wallet and could go to your place to steal things, hide out or wait for you."

"I can describe them," Josh said.

"Exactly. You can identify them. They'll want to stop you from doing that. Do you understand?" Julie asked.

Josh nodded slowly. He was now a target, in almost as much danger as Victor. But Josh had Matt close by and he was an adult. Victor was still young, even if he'd had a hard childhood.

"If it's Victor's family, they won't care about me." Josh tried to contain the fear.

"If they were beating him up, odds are it's more complicated. Was Victor selling drugs or into anything else illegal?" Julie asked.

"No, not that I know of." Josh shrugged.

Julie smiled. "We'll interview people at the shelter and search his room. Mr. Braidshaw, for now, you can't go home."

"I can call my sister," Josh relented.

"No, that would put your family at immediate risk. These men have your wallet. They can look up your name and, with the Internet, they could find your family, their address and so on. We'll have a patrol car cruise around your sister's home to be sure there is nothing suspicious, but you can't go there. I have to get back to the scene and get things started. You're acquainted with Detective Blackburn, so our Lieutenant has determined Matt will handle it from here and manage your safety," she said.

Josh looked past the pretty lady to the hunk. It sounded so final, but at least he wasn't in the hands of a stranger. Being so close to Matt might be a nice distraction, and he liked the dream. He'd fantasized plenty about Matt before. Reality was usually when guys let him down.

"I have friends too, but I don't want to put them in danger," Josh said.

"Exactly." Matt, who had walked in just at that moment and had obviously heard him, nodded to Julie. "Keep me posted."

Julie left and Matt stepped closer. "You're going to come home with me for safety, at least for tonight. We'll get some food and lockdown there until morning," Matt said.

Frowning, Josh sat up straight. "I can go the station and provide what I know now."

"We have enough to go on at this point from the initial report from the first officers on the scene. Your memory was a bit hazy and a good night's sleep will help. Things get clearer and we want as clear a picture as we can get. Odds are we'll find the car by morning."

Matt removed his jacket. "You can wear this until we get home. I can lend you some clothes."

"You don't have to. Can't we go to my place and just grab some?" Josh asked.

"It's not safe. The police will go there and secure the scene if it looks like anything was taken. I'll ask Julie to pack you a bag, if possible, but when your place is under surveillance, odds are that she won't risk it. We can hit a store in the morning." Matt handed over his jacket.

The nurse poked her head in. "Discharge papers are printing."

"Thanks," Matt said.

Josh stood slowly and shrugged on the jacket that was a bit too big for him. The smell of Matt enveloped him and he had to keep a check on his attraction. The nurse came in with papers for him to sign. Josh would've signed anything to get out, but he wasn't just going home. He was going home with Matt.

"Ready?" Matt asked.

Josh nodded. "All my stuff...my credit cards. What a mess."

"We can make those calls to cancel them. It's not a picnic, but you're alive. My job is to keep it that way." Matt led the way.

Josh followed, admiring the view. Matt looked good in the suit, but without the coat, his muscled arms were easier to admire. If they weren't in a life or death situation, Josh might have managed to tease Matt with a 'nice ass' comment. Instead, Josh said a silent prayer for Victor. Josh had to put all of his faith and his life in Matt's hands. The weirdest part was how natural it felt.

Chapter Three

Matt turned off his security alarm and got Josh into the house, along with the food they'd picked up. It felt comfortable yet oddly intimate to have this man staying over. He'd never had a witness under his protection before.

"Sorry it's a mess." Matt flipped on lights and locked the doors behind them. Turning the alarm system back on and checking the street in case they were followed from the hospital wasn't a normal habit for coming home, but Matt had never had this situation before in his career.

"I could've gone to a motel. It's a nice house," Josh said.

Matt chuckled. "Two-bedroom, two baths with a sunroom on the back. My grandparents left it to me. Grandpa was in the army, so he got the service part, but always said *'Cops never make any money, so here's a house, just in case.'* His will literally put it that way."

"Did he make a lot of money in the army?" Josh asked.

"Nah, Grandma was one of the first female pharmacists around. Grandpa retired to be a reservist then worked at the local recruiting offices and helped local ROTC groups. Sorry. I don't know why I brought them up." Matt put the food on the table. "Eat. You'll feel better. I'll get the guest room prepped."

"Matt, please... Eat and relax. I'm not a real guest." Josh grabbed Matt's hand as he sat at the wooden table, which had a lace doily under a bowl of lemons. "I'm guessing you didn't change much around here since your grandparents died."

Matt looked at the lace. "No, not in the kitchen. It felt wrong to mess with Grandma's stuff here. Grandpa could cook, but it was literally for an army. Grandma restricted him to the grilling. Cleaning out the rest of the house was hard enough, but the plates and pans still work. Plus, it's like going back in time. The living room? Sure, I changed out the TV and the couch. Bedroom? Definitely, my own set. The guest room will still feel very proper with ladylike touches, but it's comfortable enough. I haven't dusted in there in a while, though. I'm not the best housekeeper." Matt stood there, unsure as to what to do next as they sort of just held hands. It felt too easy. There had to be a catch.

"Sit and eat. Seriously, I can crash on the couch," Josh said.

"No, too exposed. Even with the curtain closed on that big picture window, they might be able to make out that someone was sleeping on the couch. I couldn't face Minnie if you got hurt worse," Matt said.

Josh smiled and released Matt's hand. "You're the boss. Your house. I can't thank you enough. Going through this with a stranger would be hell."

Matt was the one who felt exposed, having Josh in his house. In his jacket. Josh was still shirtless and Matt liked the view. "I'm happy to help. I'll get you a shirt."

Matt went to his bedroom and found an old T-shirt that was too tight for him now. He'd put on some muscle since the academy. Lots of cops got softer, but he was determined not to let that happen. Next, Matt grabbed a pair of sweatpants and clean boxers too. That was a rather intimate thing to share, but Josh had nothing here. It was sad, and yet the idea of Josh wearing his boxers, clean or not, had Matt's blood pumping extra hard.

Matt returned to the kitchen. "Here are some clothes. We'll see if Julie can get more, but I've got plenty you can borrow. The guest bath has extra stuff under the sink—a toothbrush, all of it."

"Used to having lots of men stay over?" Josh teased.

Matt cleared his throat. "Not as much as I'd like. I just like things ready. You never know when a friend will need a place to crash. Sorry... Do you want something to drink?"

"I could use a beer," Josh said.

"Oh, your pain meds. You probably shouldn't...but check." Matt went to the fridge and got two cans of soda and a pitcher of water. Then he grabbed a couple of glasses from the cabinet.

Josh took his pain meds out of the bad. "Such a goody-two-shoes. You're right. though. I shouldn't drink with those. I was just kidding. I don't think a beer would really help my head anyway. I'm okay. It's not that bad."

"You have the meds if you need them, at least." Matt sat down and pulled out the food. "Seriously, don't stress tonight. Get some rest, and in the morning, you'll feel better. It does wonders for your memory. If you get flashes and remember things overnight, write them down."

"What if my memory doesn't get better?" Josh smiled and took a bite of his sandwich.

Matt felt the urge to kiss him or at least hug him — and not just in a comforting way. Josh had always seemed to have it all together — a good job, a good heart that had him volunteering and a boyfriend everyone had said was mega-hot. It was sinking in that Josh was really available now. Somehow, Matt needed Josh to feel safe, and it was a deep pull he couldn't shake.

"No pressure... All you can do is your best. We've got the shelter info and there are teams at the scene. Maybe some shop near the scene had security cameras up? Victor may have stumbled into something that wasn't about him. We've had more cartel activity lately and that's why we've been on high alert. I dropped in on the shelter to warn them," Matt explained.

"Not because a young man was kidnapped and I was attacked?" Josh opened the can of pop and winced. "Seriously, I knew that. Minnie told me you'd been by."

Matt reached out. "If you need help, ask."

Josh smirked. "Maybe in the shower."

Matt froze for a split second. "Wherever you need."

They stared at each other for a long moment and Matt wanted to lean in. The temptation was right there and he could so easily give in to it. At work, he could keep up his control, but being this close to Josh was going to be dangerous.

Josh chuckled. "I'm a bit punchy from the meds and the stress."

Josh laughed and looked away, as did Matt.

"This is weird. No one thinks of themselves as a victim until something happens to them. You were trying to save someone, which makes you a hero, even if you didn't succeed," Matt said.

"Very much *not* a hero. These kids don't even have the decent middle-class family security I did. Volunteering is one thing, but I definitely acted on impulse. It might be normal for you, but it's weird for me. I've only ever gotten a speeding ticket," Josh said.

"You're a witness in protective custody, not in trouble. If these men are part of the cartel and you can ID them, you're in danger. If it's something else, good. I'm not downplaying what happened to you and Victor... We're just responding with a lot quickly because if it's cartel—and Victor is on the wrong side of them—the DEA will likely get involved if we can prove drugs and the cartel are involved. Then Victor is probably already dead and they'll come for you to eliminate the witnesses. I'm sorry, but that's the worst-case scenario. It could go down very fast," Matt replied.

Josh nodded. "Victor's a good kid. He was getting clean."

"Hopefully it's just a dust-up with his dealers. Maybe he owes them money. He's worth more alive than dead in that case." Matt wanted to put a good spin on things, but false hope hurt people.

"You don't believe it," Josh said. "If he was mixed up with cartel-level crap, he was trying to get out of it. I know it."

"I believe you. I have to be open to all options right now, because we don't have all the information. It's the job." Matt took a deep breath. "But if he was trying to get out of a cartel, he should've run farther away than Texas. Like...Canada."

Josh focused on eating. The place was homey, with old touches that seemed like Matt somehow, even if they conflicted with the ultra-masculine aspects. A traditional suburban life seemed so fitting, even for the gay detective.

"I didn't mean anything is wrong with Victor, but the cartel's reach is massive," Matt said.

Josh nodded. "Victor isn't even Mexican, I don't think. Not really."

"Ever hear him speak Spanish?" Matt asked.

Josh tried to remember but his head started throbbing. "Mario does. A lot of the kids do. Maybe I should take a pain pill?"

"Sorry... Don't rack your brain. We'll figure it out." Matt cleared up his trash then poured Josh a glass of water.

Opening the pill bottle, Josh glanced up and noticed a magnet on the fridge. He popped his head back and took a pill, chasing it with water, and rechecked the fridge magnet. It was for a gay club downtown. He smiled.

"You really are gay?" Josh asked.

Matt turned from the sink, his cheeks a bit pink, and walked to Josh. "Yes. Why would you think I wasn't?"

Josh shrugged. "I don't know. You never had one of those little rainbow pins a lot of uniform officers do. Officer Gay-friendly... You're the macho type. That's cool. I just didn't get the vibe off of you."

"At the job, I work. I'm gay but it doesn't change how I treat people or how I want people to treat me. I'm not good at flirting or playing games. I never did the pride parades and such. Hookups and all that? They're fine for some people, but it's a quick fix. That's not me," Matt said.

"Meaning?" Josh prompted as he kept eating. He could feel the pain pill kicking in. He didn't ache all over anymore.

"Drugs, booze, sex or whatever… People use it to numb pain, fear or loneliness. There's nothing wrong with that, in small doses, but it's not looking what I'm looking for. A lot of people use sex as a feel-good instead of dealing with their lives. That's why I like that bar. There are plenty of tables and bar stools. The dance party is upstairs, so you can just sit on the main bar level and have a drink, hear yourself think or listen to someone else talk, be social without getting groped." Matt put the pitcher of water away.

"Get groped a lot, do you?" Josh teased.

"Not with my badge on. Want dessert or something?" Matt asked.

"No thanks." Josh looked at the shiny eye-level badge. Matt's groin was also around eye level. Both aspects of Matt were very attractive.

Matt grabbed Josh's trash and disposed of it. Josh had finished his food without realizing how hungry he'd been. The stress still had him feeling a bit tingly. He was coming down off the adrenaline.

Josh took another long drink of water. "The pain pill is helping. I'm definitely feeling tired. I think I'll just crash."

"Okay." Matt grabbed the clothes and led the way down a narrow hall. "The guest bath is there on the left, the bedroom next to it. The alarm is on, so don't open windows or doors if you don't want sirens. If you need something, I'm right across the hall," Matt said.

"Thanks." Josh reach for his back pocket. "I feel so weird without my phone."

Matt patted Josh's shoulder. "We can get you a new one tomorrow, deal with the wallet stuff and we'll get an update from Julie."

Josh leaned in and hugged Matt. He smelled so good that Josh didn't want to let go. "Thanks. Like I said

Under His Protection

before, this would be much harder with a total stranger."

Matt rubbed Josh's back and held him, the comfort creating a different sort of tension in Josh.

"It's never easy," Matt offered.

Josh pulled back a bit but wanted more. Matt felt so solid, muscular and warm. He was the only thing making Josh feel safe in the world. His warmth made Josh never want to let go.

As Matt broke the hug, Josh leaned in and kissed him before the moment was gone. Matt's body was a wall of muscle and strength. He returned the kiss, but through the pain pill's tingling, Josh knew it was wrong.

Josh backed off. "Sorry. I'm...sorry." He went into the bathroom and locked the door.

Chapter Four

After a check-in with Julie, Matt spent the night going through his phone, trying not to think about that kiss and wondering how to find Victor. If he'd run from a cartel and been recaptured, he'd be dead by now.

Matt's mouth still tingled. He wanted more with Josh, but what had happened between them had been fast, probably just the shock and vulnerability mixed with pain pills. Matt didn't want to be a rebound guy either. Josh was single again, but being a victim of a crime and still in the midst of danger? People did things in that situation that they wouldn't normally.

He'd managed a few hours of decent sleep before getting up to shower. Matt dressed like it was any other day, but this case was personal.

As he walked to the kitchen for coffee, he heard the shower in the guest bathroom. Josh was up, so that was a plus.

Matt's phone rang before he even got to his first cup.

"Yeah, Jules," Matt answered.

"How's your new boyfriend?" she teased.

"Don't. He's a victim and a witness. I'm not playing games now. Did you find his wallet? His car?" Matt asked.

"No, none of the above. They swept the area with patrols and plain clothes units all night. It's like they ghosted us," Julie said.

"Sounds like cartel behavior," Matt replied.

"The shelter had photos of all their residents, so we have that picture of Victor and it's okay. But if we could get the picture of the guys who attacked him..." Julies said.

Matt sipped his coffee from his Longhorns mug. "Josh said he snapped a pic on his phone, but the phone is crushed. We can go to the cell store and see if they can transfer stuff. Maybe the SIM card is okay?"

"Try. We need something more to go on," Julie said.

"Okay. I'll be in later. We need to cancel his cards, get him an ID and so on. Call with anything," Matt replied.

"Same with you. Do me a favor and don't be a cold jerk to Josh because it's work. You might be sending a chillier message than you think." Julie hung up before Matt could reply.

Matt tossed his phone onto the counter and downed some coffee.

Josh walked in, wearing nothing but the sweatpants. Well, hopefully the boxers too, but Matt didn't try to look too closely. How could anyone call him chilly with Josh around?

"How are you feeling?" Matt asked.

"Better, I think. I slept like the dead. That pain pill... I don't usually take anything more than an ibuprofen now and then. But I'm still pretty damn sore, so I can't say it's not called for." Josh caught Matt's eye. "Sorry about the...thing."

"Forget it. We're adults. Coffee?" Matt offered.

"Please. Black is fine." Josh sat at the table. "I'm not sure I can forget it. Min put it in my head, then you weree there and taking me home. It all happened so fast."

"Min did *what*?" Matt put a mug of coffee in front of Josh.

"Nothing. Thanks." Josh took a drink. "I really hope we can go get my clothes."

"You can borrow jeans or whatever. They might not be a perfect fit, but they're clean," Matt offered.

Josh nodded and stole a look. "I appreciate it, but I'll drown in your shirts. They are fit for a bodybuilder."

Fighting off a blush, Matt cleared his throat. "Hardly, but I get wanting your own clothes."

Matt tried not to look at the piercing he'd noticed the day before. He should've been focused on a kidnapping and Josh's injuries, not the small bar through his nipple or the sexy contour of his chest.

"No luck on your car or wallet yet. Hopefully, when we get you a new phone, that picture you took will transfer over. Getting a look at the bad guys will help. How's the memory?" Matt asked.

"A bit less fuzzy, but I was looking at Victor. The other men were all in black, but I can try to give descriptions," Josh said.

Matt nodded. "We'll try the phone place first. I'm sorry that I don't have a lot of food in the house. Breakfast isn't my thing. I keep some frozen dinners and pizzas, but I hate shopping."

"Grocery shopping is a pain. I'm fine," Josh replied.

"I hate shopping, period. My aunt measured me for a wedding tux when I stood up for a friend one time. My uncle wears suits for work, so she used that info and picked out all my suits, shirts and shoes." Matt shrugged.

"She has really good taste. The suits look like they were custom-made for you." Josh looked Matt up and down. "Sorry."

"Stop apologizing. Min mentioned you're single now. I think she fancies herself a bit of a matchmaker. I'm not saying it's a bad idea or that I'm not attracted to you, but right now there's another priority." Matt poured another cup of coffee and checked his phone.

Josh folded his arms over his bare chest. "Victor and I appreciate that. Min has good taste and excellent instincts. She told me my ex was a player. I had him all wrong."

"It happens. I got sick of games and just focused on work. I don't want hook-ups and I'm not ready for adoption and a white picket fence," Matt said.

"You've already got the fence. What's in between those extremes? Live with a guy until something better comes along?" Josh asked.

"I don't know. My aunt says you know when you know and settling down is all you want, which was so helpful. At least she's not trying to set me up with every gay guy she knows. Let me see if I have some better clothes." Matt put his phone in his pocket and went into his bedroom. He had to find something for Josh other than sweats or he'd be staring at Josh's ass and-or his package every chance he got.

He returned with a pair of jeans that should fit Josh, if a bit short, but the boot-cut should cover it, and he found an old T-shirt. "These might work okay. The shirt is before I went hard at lifting in the gym."

Josh kicked off his shoes, slipped off the sweats and put on the jeans. Finally, he tugged the shirt over his head. "Way better, thanks. What made you bulk up?"

Matt relaxed again. He'd tried not to stare, but Josh's swimmer's body was worth looking at. "Bulk up? The guys at the gym don't think I'm that big. It helps with the job to look like you're formidable. You're less likely to get hit if people think you'll come back harder. And it was important if you had an ex who couldn't seem to control his temper and had to let off steam with his fists."

"Glad I'm not the only one who has had bad taste in the past. What happened?" Josh asked.

"I don't like to talk about it. But it makes it easier to be alone than to make those mistakes again. Let's go. Phone…then you can go give your statement to Jules," Matt said.

"Not you?" Josh sounded disappointed.

Matt smiled as his phone rang. "No. She's nice."

He answered his phone. "Okay, on our way."

"What? Victor?" Josh asked hopefully.

"They found your car. It's on fire." Matt led the way out of the house.

* * * *

Josh wanted to take a picture of his burning truck and send it to his insurance guy, but he still didn't have a phone. Their plan had changed when they'd heard about the truck. They had wanted to salvage what they could, but it was engulfed in flames, so that wasn't happening. He felt so stupid and out of place. He couldn't go home, he couldn't check his messages and he couldn't really make a move on Matt because he was working all the time.

Feeling this vulnerable wasn't normal for Josh. Matt's solid presence and the hint of a cologne Josh wanted to smell more of helped. Still, Josh wanted to go home, go to work and take Matt on a date.

Is this real? Josh stood there in another man's clothes, next to that man, who he'd kissed the night before. He knew it wasn't the fear or the painkillers, but he wanted Matt. The attraction had always been there, but he'd wasted time on Bill.

Matt and Josh hadn't had much of a chance to be alone before. There had always been shelter stuff with teens around or Min and other staff buzzing about. The more Josh grew to know Matt, the more he understood that Matt had an old-fashioned work ethic and sensibility. It only magnified the manly nature that was no joke.

Writing it off as a weak moment with Matt had been easy, but Josh wanted what he'd done on impulse to happen again. He wanted Matt to kiss him back and take him to the master bedroom. Matt was just his type. His manliness was intoxicating. Josh had a domestic and caretaking side that had brought him to the shelter, yet he couldn't find a good guy to play house with.

"We'll get a report that you can send to your insurance company," Matt offered.

Josh nodded. "Can you take a picture of that for the insurance? I want to get a rental as soon as possible."

Matt took the picture. "You don't need a car right now. You're stuck with me, under my protection. I'm not letting you go rogue."

Josh smiled. Matt would say things that sounded sweet then correct himself to the professional-sounding answer. That told Josh it wasn't just him feeling an attraction.

"Can we get the phone now?" Josh asked.

"No, back to the station. I want to talk to him now," Julie said.

"We haven't even had breakfast. We'll grab lunch and meet you there," Matt suggested.

"We'll order in from the diner and eat while we talk," Julie countered.

Matt nodded. Josh was starving, but he'd rather be alone with Matt, where he could feel safe and pretend the rest of this wasn't really happening.

But Victor was still missing and bad guys had all of Josh's most sensitive info. "Damn."

"What's wrong?" Matt asked.

"My social security card was in my wallet. I never took that card out, even though I know I should have. Damn..." Josh cursed himself.

"We can put you in touch with people who protect and restore identities for a living. It's not easy, but they can do it," Matt said.

"You just have an answer for everything." Josh smirked.

"I try. You're alive. The rest can be handled. They have patrols checking your sister's neighborhood, the shelter, your work and your home. We'll catch these guys. Let's get to the station, then we can get the phone on the way home. You'll feel more normal — if you can remember all your passwords," Matt said.

"That's mean." Josh nudged Matt playfully. "If they transfer my account, all that should be programmed in properly."

"At least I made you smile," Matt said.

* * * *

A statement, a phone and an insurance call later, Josh didn't have a rental car but the process had been started. He also had a bag of clothes an officer had grabbed for him from his place. Thus far, no one had tried to break in, and that was the only really good news.

"I'll order a pizza and we should just beat it there," Matt said.

"I can cook. I owe you a home-cooked meal, at least," Josh offered.

Matt shook his head. "I'm doing my job. This isn't a favor for Min...or a date."

Josh felt the chill settle in. "Fine. Pizza. Veggie is fine...or just cheese." Josh had most of his passwords memorized and he logged in to Twitter and Insta, plus his emails.

"I'm sorry. I didn't mean it like that. You've been through a lot. The last thing you need to do is work or worry about my food choices."

"I understand. We've been around each other before but never alone for a long time. I like it. I know it's work and it's not a normal date, but hopefully we'll have a chance to do that when the case is over," Josh suggested.

"Hopefully. Got the picture?" Matt got on his own phone and texted while they sat at a red light. "Pizza ordered."

"You're driving. You're not supposed to be on your phone," Josh teased.

"I'll give myself a warning. Now that you've got a phone, do you have the photo or not?" Matt pushed as he changed lanes and took a detour while keeping an eye on the rearview mirror.

Josh changed to the photos app. "Yes! Crap."

"Is it blurry?" Matt drove along as the light turned green then pulled a quick U-turn.

"What's wrong?" Josh asked.

Matt shook his head. "Nothing. I just wanted to make sure we weren't being followed. We're fine. Is the picture bad?"

Josh chuckled. "No, but I forgot I have cloud backup. I could've logged into it at any time and seen the pics. I'm an idiot, but I'm glad we're not being followed."

"No, no one thought about that possibility. This isn't your fault," Matt reminded Josh with a pat on the leg.

The electricity of the touch made Josh tense. They should wait and be professional, but it was hard to follow the rules.

"If I had gone another way home, maybe he'd have handled it? Maybe he'd be okay?" Josh scrolled through missed calls. He texted his sister back that there was a work emergency and he needed to be unavailable for a bit, helping a patient.

"Don't do that." Matt whipped his SUV into the driveway and parked it. He leaned over. "You are the only reason we even know Victor was in danger. No one else in that neighborhood would've reported the fight. He was too far from the shelter, so no one saw a thing. A nineteen-year-old guy going missing from a shelter? He's an adult. Min would've had to wait forty-eight hours before anyone would've even taken a report. Victor can go where he wants and without any proof he's in danger. Those are the cases that slip through the cracks. No family or girlfriend would have been nagging at the police."

"Squeaky wheel," Josh said.

"And overburdened, understaffed police. Missing kids get the most attention, then seniors and women. It's that old stigma that men can take care of themselves. Send me the pic. If Victor makes it out of this alive, it's because of you." Matt leaned over and kissed Josh hard and quick.

Josh tried to extend the kiss, but a knock on the window made them jump.

"Pizza," the guy said.

* * * *

Josh ate pizza and organized his new phone. At least he had some things that were his now. Matt was on his phone, talking with Julie about the picture. When Matt was finally done with the call, he began checking emails.

"You better eat something," Josh said.

Matt sighed and grabbed a slice. "We need a break."

"We could try going to my place. We could swing by the shelter and scene of the crime," Josh suggested.

"You're not bait," Matt countered.

Josh sipped a beer. "I don't mind, if it'll help Victor."

"It might not." Matt grabbed himself a beer from the fridge.

"Do we wait for it to blow over? Am I your new roomie?" Josh teased.

Matt finally cracked a smile. "The problem is, two more shootings were reported today. No kidnappings, but there were two dead guys. Narcotics guys are on it, but it might be related."

"You don't have to babysit me. Go do your job," Josh said.

"Babysitting the eyewitness is my job right now. It's frustrating, but we all play our part. I'm lucky I got the hot-guy duty." Matt chuckled as he leaned against the counter and downed more of his beer.

Josh put down the pizza and wiped his hands. Walking over to Matt, he knew it could be a big mistake…

"Sorry you're stuck with me and frustrated with the job. Or are you annoyed that we didn't finish that kiss in the car?" Josh asked.

Before Matt could answer, Josh kissed him. He was ready for anything from a shove to a punch when he furthered the kiss, but Matt did neither. He pulled Josh in and steered them toward the master bedroom.

Josh stripped out of Matt's clothes and yanked Matt's shirt open. Buttons flew.

"Sorry," Josh said.

Matt chuckled. "I'm not…" Matt didn't finish the sentence but went in for another kiss. Josh enjoyed the firm touch as Matt ran his hands down Josh's chest and around to grab his ass. The taste of beer and pizza only added to his arousal. They both needed this.

Going for Matt's belt, Josh knelt down.

Matt groaned as Josh sucked the long cock into his mouth. Was Matt happy about the blow job or sad because of the kiss? Josh felt it would likely be a mix of both. Most guys he'd been with lately were more interested in sex, and Matt was a damn good kisser. Josh wanted more of it all.

Nudging Matt back onto the bed, Josh followed, totally naked. Once Matt was good and hard, Josh came up for air. "Got protection?"

Matt rummaged around the nightstand and produced a few condoms. "Damn, I'm out of lube."

Josh smirked. Matt might not last very long. "Whatever… I'm up for anything."

Josh licked his way down Matt's hard body and sucked the cock from the fantasy he'd had about Matt more than a few times. Matt's grunts and groans only made his own erection strain even more.

When Josh tried to kiss his way up Matt's torso, Matt flipped him flat on his back like a trapped suspect. Josh wouldn't mind if he'd whip out some handcuffs, but no such luck.

Matt did suck Josh's dick down to his balls, however. *The guy has no gag reflex?* Josh panted and thrust upward. The noises Matt made encouraged Josh, and he sat up so he could reach around and smack Matt's round ass. Muscle was everywhere on this guy, but not in an overdone steroid-jock way.

When Matt didn't push Josh's hand away, Josh took the hint and smacked that ass again. Matt moaned. Josh grabbed a handful of flesh and let his fingers tease Matt's asshole. The hyper-masculine cop was complicated, and it made Josh come faster than he'd ever expected. He cursed and said Matt's name way too many times for a first round in bed.

He wanted there to be more, but Matt pulled away.

"You're hard again." Josh grabbed Matt's cock.

"Don't." Matt didn't pull away as Josh jerked his dick.

"We need it. Forget everything else," Josh said.

Matt looked Josh in the eye. Josh rolled Matt onto his back and kept stroking him. Matt slid his hand behind Josh's head, but instead of shoving his face toward that gorgeous dick, Matt pulled him up. Sinking into the deep kiss, Josh pressed his whole body to Matt's. Only their mouths and Josh's one hand moved. It felt like slow motion, but Josh wanted to remember every second of the hottest hand job he'd ever given in his life.

Chapter Five

Matt slipped from the warm bed and into the shower. He could smell Josh, who'd been curled up next to him all night, but it was wrong. Maybe it wasn't the wrong guy, but it was definitely the completely wrong time.

Josh had just gotten the crap beat out of him and watched a kid he'd mentored be kidnapped. Sure, Josh needed protection and to feel safe, but no matter who had instigated it, Matt should've been able to resist.

Sex with a person in police protective custody? If that got out, Matt would be written up, investigated and lucky to keep his job. Julie had meant well, nudging them together, but timing... Wrong timing could ruin what otherwise might work. Josh was more vulnerable than normal, whether he admitted it or not.

Matt got ready for work while Josh was in the guest shower. Somehow, he made it to the kitchen without running into Josh in the small house. Butterflies weren't something Matt normally had to deal with. He'd learned to block fear, but this was different. When Josh walked into the kitchen, Matt felt like he'd swallowed a field full of butterflies.

"Coffee?" Matt offered.

"Thanks. Look—" Josh began.

"I'm sorry. It shouldn't have happened," Matt blurted out.

Josh froze for a second then nodded. "Okay. We gave it a shot."

"No, I was totally out of line," Matt tried to explain.

Josh shook his head. "How? I kissed you first. I certainly didn't object."

"I probably reinjured your ribs. That's the last thing you should be doing while healing." Matt's phone rang.

He answered it, grateful for the distraction. "Hey, Julie."

"I left my phone charging. I'll get it," Josh said.

Matt nodded to Josh. Since he was in the middle of a case, Matt had his mind on the work, and all he wanted to do was solve the case so he could think about Josh. Maybe then they could have a fair shot.

Who'd come on to whom or consent wasn't the point. Josh was a victim of a crime. Matt wanted to hate himself, but he didn't regret it, not deep down where he should.

As Julie was rattling on about the updates from overnight, Matt heard the front door open and close. The butterflies left and cold dread took their place.

"Hang on, Jules," Matt said as he walked to the front in time to see Josh in the back of a hired car as it pulled away. "Damn. Josh got a Lyft or something and just left."

"Follow him!" Julie shouted.

"Relax. I'm on it. I know where he's headed." Matt paused at the door to see if anyone else reacted.

One car that was parked down the street started up and headed in the same direction that Josh's hired car had just gone.

"I need backup and a SWAT team to the shelter." He hung up and headed for his car.

* * * *

Having the Lyft driver take him by the crime scene made Josh feel guilty. The tape was down and people were going on about their lives like it was nothing. He didn't see anything suspect, but it was early in the morning. *Bad guys only come out at night, right?*

"Is this it?" the driver asked.

"No, I want to keep going to the shelter. I just wanted to drive by here," Josh said.

"Hey, it's your money." The driver proceeded to the shelter and Josh used his cash app, which had been thankfully uncompromised, to pay for the ride.

He walked into the shelter and Min nearly tackled him.

"You're safe." She hugged him.

"Any news on Victor?" he asked.

She released him and shook her head. "Lots of cops asking lots of questions, but nothing else. We've had a lot of patrol cars around, so some of the drop-in kids are staying away. Where's Matt?"

"I slipped away. It got weird," Josh said.

"Weird good? I know you were in protective custody," she teased.

"I also have two broken ribs and a fair amount of bruising—and I'm his case, not his boyfriend," Josh added.

"Sorry. All business," Min said.

Josh shrugged. "Not really, but maybe that's it."

"Maybe that's what?" Min asked.

"We did some stuff. He apologized this morning. I'm not sure if he took pity on me last night or if he broke some police rule." Josh took a deep breath and his chest ached.

"Pity? Please. Rule are rules and you were assaulted. Let him know you weren't taken advantage of." She winked. "Unless you were…"

"No, I thought I let him know that, but he's sort of difficult to read and very hard to pin down for a real talk. But he's on a case," Josh replied.

"Trying to find Victor for you, and you're part of the case. Complicated," Min agreed.

"Do you buy this cartel crap?" Josh asked.

Min frowned. "Victor has no family around here that we could find. The guy can pass for white, but with dark eyes and hair, he might be part Mexican and keeps it to himself. We don't care, but he might be trying to blend in to get away. If ICE picks him up, he's screwed. Plenty of kids try to escape a bad situation."

"Any weird cars around here?" Josh asked.

"Always. But no one has gotten shot at. We're keeping things quiet. Everyone is staying inside, residents only, no events or anything. But they are doing their AA meetings." Min nodded.

The kids were watching through her office window.

Josh walked out and to where they were. "Hey, I'm fine."

"Victor?" Mario asked.

"No word yet. But I snuck away from the police to make sure you guys are doing okay." Josh patted kids on their shoulders.

"Looks like a bunch of cars are pulling up, a few squad cars. They found you, Josh," Min teased.

Matt had parked and was headed for the shelter entrance. Josh told the kids to hang inside. He headed out to take the threat away.

"Get back in there," Matt ordered as he stepped in.

"What's going on?" Josh asked.

"A car followed you from my place this morning. I'm not sure why they did or who they are. I followed them to this neighborhood but backed off so they didn't realize they were being tailed. Backup and SWAT are coming, but you need to stay inside," Matt instructed.

Josh pushed Matt back toward the door. "No, we need to go. We have to get them away from the kids."

"Josh, the car is parked out front. I have the plates and the description. They saw me walk in here. They know that we know," Matt explained as they walked farther inside.

"What do they want?" Minnie asked, clearly having heard their exchange.

"Josh dead, most likely, to keep him from identifying the guys who took Victor," Matt replied.

"I should've listened to you and stayed put," Josh whispered.

Matt's phone beeped.

SWAT team activated.

"Get down, away from the front," Matt ordered everyone.

The SWAT team swarmed the car that had followed Josh. It appeared to be empty now. Matt watched as the police cleared each vehicle on the street. Before they got too far, another seemingly empty car from halfway down the block burst to life.

Two guys with semi-automatic guns opened fire on the shelter. Josh ran up, trying to pull Matt back but felt a sting.

The SWAT team swooped in and surrounded the car, but a third man slipped out of the back seat before it was fully contained. Matt took off in pursuit.

"Matt, wait!" Josh called.

"Josh, you're bleeding!" Min shouted. "Everyone back to the kitchen area, and grab the first-aid kit on the way."

Matt wanted to turn and take care of Josh, but he wasn't a doctor. He was a cop. He had a bullet-proof vest on, unlike Josh, who had tried to play hero when he wasn't armed or outfitted.

Knowing the area was an advantage. Matt followed the guy down a dead-end alley and pulled his gun. "Freeze."

The guy tried to scale the fence but Matt shot him in the leg. "Get down."

"We're both dead, stupid!" the guy shouted.

Matt shook his head. "Where's Victor?"

"Dead, now that those guys have been taken by the police," the guy replied.

"What cartel are you with? Is Victor with his family now in Mexico?" Matt asked.

The guy laughed. "Victor's not ours. He's leverage."

Matt recognized the guy's largely Tejano accent. "You're Tijuana cartel? Where is Victor from?"

"He's the grandson of one of the leaders of another cartel. We've been negotiating. The kid took off and there's a reward on his head. We could ransom him and get a very favorable negotiation without as much blood and death." The guy smiled. "But now he'll be a corpse. My guys are dead for nothing."

"Maybe…maybe not. If Victor's alive, we have some talking to do. Call your boss and see," Matt said.

"Who are you? *Jefe*?" the guy asked. "No cartel will trust us if we're in bed with Americans."

"Not even for your safety in America and witness protection for your guys who are alive? Seems like those stakes are different. Tell your guys not to kill him for now." Matt held the guy at gunpoint. There were limited options, but if Victor was alive, they had to try to get him back.

Matt had to bring in the negotiators and narcotics unit, who understood cartels and how to get trusted deals through. He'd be on the sidelines for this, but if Victor was alive, it'd mean everything to Josh.

Radioing for the proper support, Matt wanted to ask about Josh's status, but he had to focus on the case first. It could be bad news, and he couldn't handle it if Josh hadn't made it.

* * * *

For the second time in a week, Josh found himself in the ER—this time to get stitches for a gunshot wound. The bullet had caught him in the shoulder—no surgery, nothing major—but it looked awful and hurt like a bitch.

Min fussed over the kids, who had been brought in for a once-over, to be sure they were all okay. Josh tried to look calm and in control for the kids, but he was terrified. Matt had just run off after a bad guy and no one knew what had happened.

Julie paced the area. It'd been nearly an hour since Josh had arrived. He kept staring at the clock then the door and alternating like he could will Matt to come through safe and sound. When Julie got on the phone, Josh tensed up and his blood pressure spiked. He really wanted an update, but no one was talking.

"You okay?" Min came over.

"Where's Matt? He could be dead and it's all my fault," Josh said.

"He couldn't keep you in protective custody forever—or have watched you closer. You're the one who slipped away." Min patted his uninjured shoulder.

"Yep, it's all my fault. I need a drink or something," Josh said.

"No, do you need more pain meds?" Min asked.

"Just some water," Josh replied. Suddenly the kids all started chattering and went down the hall. Min followed them.

Josh grabbed his IV—a silly precaution—and joined the party.

Victor looked like hell, but he sat on a gurney...safe, breathing.

Matt stood next to him, still hot in his suit, but the tie was gone and his collar was open, revealing a bit of the bulletproof vest. His suit coat was missing too.

Min hugged Victor, but Josh rushed for Matt and held on to him. Matt hugged Josh tight and kissed his neck. "I'm okay."

"What the hell happened?" Josh asked.

"The department made a deal." Matt reached into his pants pocket. "We got your wallet back too."

"How?" Josh crushed Matt with another hug.

Julie walked up. "Got a call. The US Marshall is on the way for Victor."

"Thanks." Victor shook Matt's hand then hugged Josh. "I'm sorry."

"What for?" Josh asked.

"I have work to do. It's okay. Victor will be safe in witness protection after he gives up what he knows. The kidnappers got the same deal." Matt shrugged. "A different cartel wanted Victor for ransom or leverage. Victor didn't want to go with either of them. The kidnappers wanted a deal when they heard Victor could get one. We get massive intel on both cartels and these guys get out of that life."

"How do they know it's not just getting inside our system?" Josh asked.

Matt smiled. "That's not our call. I brought in our narcotics team and negotiators. They brought in the DEA and Marshalls. Ultimately, the Feds were willing to roll the dice. This stuff happens fast, so the Feds can move them before anyone else in the cartel gets suspicious. They'll all be watched very carefully. Victor, say your goodbyes. You won't be allowed contact with anyone from here ever again. You won't be allowed to travel to Mexico *or* Texas."

Victor nodded. "I wanted out of the cartel life anyway. I'll never find such good friends. You saved my life."

Josh patted his arm. "You're sure this is what you want?"

Victor smiled. "A chance for real life in America? Legally? No drugs and no fear? It's everything."

"Good. Go on... Say goodbye to Min and everyone. Stay clean," Josh advised.

"Yes, sir." Victor moved off to say his goodbyes to the others from the shelter.

"You're okay?" Josh asked Matt.

Matt pulled out his keychain. "Sure. All part of the job. Here... I'll tell you more at home. If you want, of course. You don't have to. Jules has to take you to the station and get your statement, but then someone can give you a ride to my place. I hope I won't be too long. Once the Feds take over, I still have to file my report and detail everything, since I was alone in pursuit for a while. Some cartel people might be sniffing around, but the conflict is between the cartels now. We'll pull the BOLO and report that Victor is believed to have returned to Mexico to his family, which is much farther south than Tijuana. For you, it's done, but it might be good not to go back to your place for a few days, to be sure it's all safe."

Taking the key, Josh felt a tingle of hope. He leaned in and kissed Matt. He wanted to be calm and cool like Matt, but Josh just couldn't help it. Matt pulled him in and returned the kiss. The shelter kids hooted and hollered, and Matt blushed.

"Sorry... I didn't mean to do that in front of your colleagues," Josh admitted.

"It's okay. But I'll have a bit more explaining to do." Matt winked.

Chapter Six

Four hours later, Josh heard Matt finally pulling up in front of the house.

Sitting on the couch watching TV and sipping a soda, Josh felt right at home. He put down the soda and stood up, one arm in a sling, when Matt came through the door.

"I'm glad you're here," Matt said as he locked the door firmly behind him.

"You're sure? I know a lot happened today, but I'm not under protective custody anymore," Josh said.

Matt smiled. "I know, and I'm glad we can talk and not have that out there anymore. It might seem dumb, because we knew each other before, but I love my job as much as you love yours. Jules smoothed it all over so I'm not in trouble, but you will probably get teased a bit if you come to any fundraisers or police events with me. Now, what's with the car? And I smell food."

"I rented a car so I'm mobile again. With my wallet back, it was easier. I did stop and get some groceries so we don't starve tonight. It's just a chicken dish. It'll be ready soon, but it'll keep if you want to do something else." Josh wanted to grab Matt and hug him—kiss him. "You're okay?"

Matt took off his coat, set down his gun and sighed. "I'm fine. I don't want you to leave."

"I know a lot happened today. But you ran into the hands of a drug cartel for Victor." Josh moved closer.

"It's my job. I did it as much for you as for Victor— keeping everyone safe. At least he'll be away from all of that cartel life. But this morning... I know you're tough and you care about these kids, but getting beat up? Hell, you got shot today. You're an addiction counselor, not a cop. You're vulnerable and you didn't even have a vest on. It was not the time to make a move. I'm sorry," Matt said.

Josh smiled. "I made the move in the ER. You didn't seem to mind."

Matt shrugged. "No, but we have to be in this for the right reasons. Julie or Min or both... They put it in our heads that we should be a couple. It wasn't the right time or circumstances."

"Life doesn't always hand us the perfect scenario. Do you regret what we did?" Josh moved into Matt's personal space. He could smell the man's sweat mixed with a faint, lingering hint of cologne.

"Not really. I wish I did. The only thing I truly regret is that I was so weird this morning. But was it real, or was it just a distraction to feel good? Feel safe? Pain pills mixed with fear and adrenaline?" Matt asked.

The oven buzzer went off. Josh turned. "Do you mind getting the food? It's easier with two hands, especially when it's hot."

Matt found a dish towel and used it for oven mitts. Quickly setting the glass dish on the counter, he took a deep breath. "Smells great. You're not going to answer me?"

"Let's talk over dinner." Josh had set the table. He grabbed his soda while Matt got himself a beer.

Matt served the food, then both of them settled at the table.

"My ex was a jerk who played people. I thought we clicked and it took months to realize he was someone else to everyone else. He'd be a man's man with me then flirty at bars. He was flamboyant at work, so everyone knew he was gay and no one wanted to be accused of discrimination. He was loyal when he was sober and cheated like it was normal to have an orgy when he drank," Josh said.

"I'm sorry you went through that. My last boyfriend couldn't handle the strain of my job. My work is dangerous. Then again, so is your volunteering," Matt said.

Josh shrugged and nodded. "I always liked you, but somewhere in my head I thought you'd probably be just like him—a tough cop at work, maybe someone totally different at home and someone else with your fam or friends. I don't regret anything, because you were truthful about who and what you are. But don't feel like you have to like me because you had to protect me."

"I would never do that. You had a boyfriend when we met and for a good year or so after. I'm not a home wrecker." Matt took a bite of dinner. "This is great."

Josh ate a bit too. "Thanks, and I'm glad you like it. What I've seen from being in your custody is that you're you. You don't change. You don't lie or fake anything. That is the sexiest thing I've ever seen in a man."

"Are you sure that's not the rebound feelings talking?" Matt asked.

"God no. That relationship has been over for quite some time. I didn't want to go on the dating circuit again—or have hookups. I want someone in my life who gets it, who gets me. Min was right." Josh ate his dinner.

"Give it a month and you'll hate that I'm a cop," Matt said.

"Don't tell me what I'll hate. I've had addicts try to punch, scratch, kick and bite me. I've had kids from that shelter try to slip me GHB or grab me and kiss me. We've had dealers arrested for being on rehab property or the shelter. You know as well as I do that all that activity could be gang-related and bring more trouble later. My work might not be as relentlessly dangerous, but you'll worry as much as I will." Josh grabbed another soda from the fridge and bumped his arm. "Damn."

"Did you take the pain meds?" Matt asked.

"No, I wanted a clear head. I'm fine." Josh sat back down.

"Why addiction counseling?" Matt asked.

"My dad was a drunk, and once he got sober, he was a good guy—not perfect, but good. It just so happens that I'm good at managing people with addictions. Hopefully I can go back to work next week, even with the sling," Josh said.

Matt grabbed his phone. "What's your ex's name? Bill something?"

"What? You're going to check my story?" Josh asked.

"No, but if he gets pulled over or arrested, I can make damn sure they give him hell. Cops stick together," Matt said.

"You'll harass him for me? How sweet," Josh teased. "I should be able to go home tonight. You don't have to put me up."

Matt stood up. "If you want to go, I won't stop you, but would you really feel safe?"

Josh walked up to Matt. "Is it about feeling safe? Or do you want me here?"

Matt stared at Josh. "I want you here, but you were just shot. I've never even been shot. That's not something you just power through. I want you to be here with me because you want to, not for safety or sex. I want you safe and I want sex, but not just that. I think I need another beer. I'm not great at talking about feelings."

"What's wrong with starting like this? Building from here? I didn't get shot in the head. I know what I'm doing. What aren't you telling me?" Josh asked.

"I'm what you see. Whatever you called it, hyper-masculine. True. But that isn't exactly what I'm into in…" Matt opened a beer and took a sip.

"The bedroom stuff? That's okay. I'm not looking for a power top. I want a man with consistent character and standards, but in bed, things can be more flexible." Josh grinned.

"You're sure?" Matt's face was burning.

"If you're going to spend the rest of your life with someone, you have to be creative. Keeps things hot," Josh teased.

Matt laughed. "Wow, you did take some pain pills."

"No, I'm just very positive about us. Julie seems smart. Min is a good judge of character. We got along under that intense stress, so let's see how we get along without it. I think I'd rather stay here anyway, if that's okay. Going home, I'd feel very alone and like a target still. Being with you feels right in every possible way." Josh tried to unbutton Matt's shirt, but one-handed, things were tricky.

Matt unbuttoned his own shirt and tossed it aside. "You really want to do this with one arm in a sling?"

Josh kissed Matt slowly until Matt pulled him in hard and tangled their tongues.

"I made dinner one-handed. I can screw your brains out with no hands if I have to." Josh nudged Matt in the direction of the bedroom.

Matt yanked Josh's clothes off. "You're right. I think you'd better stay here—and give up that apartment. Once you get your insurance check for the car, we can get you something new."

"Shopping really doesn't get me hot," Josh replied.

"I hate shopping, but you'd be amazed how the glimpse of a badge gets salesmen to be extra nice," Matt promised.

Josh laughed. "I think you just want me to screw you in the back of brand-new pickup truck."

"Absolutely." Matt kissed him. "How the hell did I fall in love on a case? It's unprofessional and reckless."

"Yes, but you made me fall in love with you too, so it all works out. Just don't do it again. You're all mine." Josh tugged at the bulletproof vest.

"Fair is fair. Now, what did you have in mind for dessert?" Matt asked, after kissing his way down Josh's neck.

"Oh, I didn't make anything. My shoulder started to hurt. I guess you'll have to be dessert for me — and vice versa," Josh taunted.

"Just what I had in mind." Matt eased Josh back toward the master bedroom. He wanted to keep Josh forever — safe, happy and all his.

TICKET TO FREEDOM

ELIZABETH HOLLOWS

Dedication

To the friends who read this every word of the way.
And to my editor, Jamie Rose. I don't know where
this story would be without your help and skill.

Chapter One

Calvin Hughes opened the alleyway door with gritted teeth and a shudder. It closed behind him and he took in a grateful breath of clean air. Well, cleaner air. It was free from cigarette smoke and alcohol fumes, but there was a large, overflowing bin next to him. Calvin curled his lip and stood as far away from it as possible. He didn't lean up against the damp wall, choosing instead to stare out at the street. Neon lights bathed the busy sidewalk in red, blue and green.

The neighborhood was more than sleazy. It was downright criminal.

Calvin worked in a dive bar that was a front for all manner of illegal dealings, but he didn't get involved. He kept his head down and poured drinks. People who paid too much attention or spoke out of turn ended up with bruises and broken bones. Sometimes they disappeared entirely. It wasn't the life or career he wanted, but he had been down on his luck and desperate for a job. The bar had hired him when no one else would. Three years ago, Calvin hadn't known what dangers lurked in the shadows. Now he did, but he was stuck. He wanted to quit but was fearful of what would happen to him if he did.

He was lucky the patrons liked to fondle the waitresses rather than the quiet man behind the bar. He didn't even advertise that he was gay. Calvin didn't want to catch the eye of a criminal who would take his sexuality as an open invitation. Luckily, there weren't many handsome men to interest him. The few attractive ones were arrogant, cruel or unquestionably straight.

Calvin had given up hoping for a knight in shining armor years ago. He was trapped, and no one would rescue him.

Sighing, Calvin looked up at the sky. It was overcast and there was too much light pollution to see the stars. He missed the country. He'd grown up in a small town in the middle of nowhere. He could remember his childhood — his father coming home from work and sweeping his mother into a kiss. She'd laugh and whack him gently, telling him off for dirtying her clothes with grease from the cars and tractors he fixed. Despite her complaints, love was always shining from her eyes. His father would then wash up before hoisting Calvin into his arms to take him into the backyard to play. On his tenth birthday, the three of them had camped in the yard and looked up at the constellations. That was a year before his father had died. What he wouldn't give for a one-way ticket back to that simple, happy time — or even a one-way ticket to anywhere but here, somewhere with a small house, a loving dog, maybe even a loving husband who would sweep *him* into an affectionate embrace. He could dream.

And, that was what Calvin did on his five-minute breaks. He daydreamed about the perfect life—a man wrapping his warm, strong arms around him and kissing him breathless, nights of passion in bed and mornings spent cooking together, a home shared in love, creating a family. He could easily picture the man. His perfect lover would be taller than him, muscled and handy around the house. He'd be the blond, boy-next-door type who helped old ladies across the street, the kind of guy who would cook romantic dinners and make all his dreams come true. The images of marital bliss were sweet, even if they made the bar seem darker and gloomier by comparison.

Sighing again, Calvin glanced at his watch. It didn't pay to be late in a place like this. He was lucky he had a break at all. His bosses didn't care much about worker's rights.

Calvin let go of his fantasy man with regret and turned back to the door. He reached for the handle but flinched away at the muffled sounds of shouting and a gunshot. His blood ran cold, but before he could react, the door burst open and someone collided with him. Calvin grabbed onto the man to keep his footing, only narrowly avoiding falling to the ground. He looked down at the man in his arms. He was brunet and few inches shorter than Calvin. *Felix.* He was one of the few handsome faces Calvin ever saw. He didn't treat the waitstaff like dirt and had an infectious smile.

Felix had been coming into the club for the last month and a half. He ordered a beer but never drank it. He flirted with the barmaids and schmoozed with the owners. Calvin had seen him exchanging money. He'd also been part of private meetings in the back room. Felix wasn't deep into the illegal dealings, but he'd been worming his way into the inner circle. Felix was a young, up-and-rising criminal star. Calvin stayed away from people like that, no matter how attractive they were in a well-tailored suit. *And he is kind of handsome, though certainly not a boy-next-door. He never paid any attention to me, either, so he must be straight. He was nice to me, though, when a lot of these thugs aren't – not that I want to even consider a criminal for a partner.*

Felix's suit was in disarray now and his blue eyes were almost wild. The door had slammed shut behind him, but they both ducked when a new shot was fired. It penetrated the door but missed them. *Shit. What the hell is going on?*

Felix yanked Calvin farther down the alley and away from the door. He let Calvin go when they turned a corner but he didn't stop running. Calvin raced after him. They sprinted behind the buildings and past two exits to the street. Felix kept going until they reached a narrow road with a parked car. Calvin could still hear shouting, screaming and running footsteps. They seemed to be echoing all around them. Felix unlocked the car and jumped inside. Calvin didn't think about what he was doing. He just yanked open the passenger door then climbed in.

"What the hell?" Felix shouted. "Get out of here!"

He threw something on the backseat, but before Calvin could react, another gunshot from behind shattered the back windshield. Calvin cried out and ducked. The car roared to life and they tore out onto the street. Calvin snapped up his head, yelping with terror when they narrowly avoided a collision with another car. Felix didn't blink, skidding the tires and twisting the wheel to make it through without a scratch, then put his foot down on the accelerator, flying at three times the speed limit and weaving in and out of cars like a maniac.

Calvin's heart was pounding and he was ready to be sick by the time they screeched onto the main highway. The dive bars and nightclubs were disappearing, but Felix didn't slow down. He kept checking the rearview and side mirrors, likely to make sure they weren't being followed. Calvin panted and tried to calm his racing heart. It wasn't working.

He didn't know what was going on, but Calvin had the sinking suspicion he shouldn't have climbed into this car. He turned and looked behind him. Glass from the shattered window littered the backseat. Another item rested on the cushioning and Calvin's eyes widened.

"You stole the hard drive," he whispered.

Calvin had only seen the hard drive four times, but he would know it anywhere.

Whenever the bar was short-staffed or the waitresses had gone home, Calvin took drinks to the back room of the club. Calvin tried to be inconspicuous while he was there and just presented drinks to the table of men playing cards. It was a simple activity that masked horrible intentions. Only the top men and women were invited to that game. Murders and drug deals were planned in that room, and once in a while, a black laptop rested on the table. Calvin didn't want to know what information was on it. Illegal bank accounts? Payments to hitmen? The number of options was endless. There was always a hard drive plugged into the computer. It was a small silver one with a scratch in the corner.

It was the same hard drive that rested under broken glass on Felix's back seat. He turned back to find Felix clenching the steering wheel and gritting his teeth.

"You stole the hard drive," Calvin said again, his voice growing louder and threaded with panic.

"Why the hell did you get in my car?" Felix snapped. "What the hell were you doing?"

Calvin hadn't been thinking and that was the problem. Felix had pulled him away from the door and the gunshots. He'd assumed Felix would be safe or at least unconnected with what was going on in the club. He'd been wrong.

Now Calvin was in a car with the man everyone wanted to see dead. He was guilty by association.

I'm screwed.

"Well?" Felix demanded, glancing away from the road to glare at him. "Got any more stupid ideas?"

Calvin bristled at the insult.

"You pulled me away from the door! How was I supposed to know you were the one they were shooting at?"

"What kind of idiot jumps into a car with a stranger?"

"What kind of idiot steals a hard drive from a criminal empire?"

Felix clenched his jaw but didn't respond. Calvin was still breathing heavily, adrenaline pumping through his veins and making his hands tremble. He turned away from Felix to stare out of the window. They were still in the city with cars, buildings and people all around them. It didn't comfort him.

Where is Felix taking us? Where is he taking the hard drive?

There were hundreds of rival gangs and organizations that would love to have that hard drive. Calvin might turn a blind eye to what happened around him, but he wasn't stupid. He'd seen the aftermath of drive-by shootings when a new group tried to muscle in on the empire's territory. He'd seen the terrified faces of people in his apartment block when the racketeers came calling. Calvin knew how much money and property was at stake if the information on that hard drive was leaked, so he also knew how much blood could be spilled by the guys trying to get it back.

How much danger am I in right now? Is Felix going to silence me before I can talk to anyone?

Calvin knew it was useless, but as the terror took hold again, he found words tumbling out of him.

"I won't tell anyone if you let me go. They won't know anything, I swear."

Felix startled, seeming surprised by his statement. "Let you *go*? You'll be dead within hours if I let you go."

A cold shiver of fear ran down Calvin's spine. It was one thing to think it, another to hear it.

"I don't want you here," Felix continued, "but I can't just throw you out."

"Why not?" Calvin asked, feeling confused. "What does it matter to you?"

"Because, it, well…" Felix swore under his breath. "Look…" he continued. "I'm not going to let you get shot because of me, okay?"

The sentiment was simple but unexpected from a criminal. His actions didn't make sense either. He'd yanked Calvin away from gunfire when he could have left him to die. It was the decent and heroic thing to do.

But why would an out-for-himself criminal do that? Why does Felix give a damn about me? Anyone else at the bar would have run away without a second glance. They would have kicked him out of the car to fend for himself—but not Felix. It didn't add up.

Who is this man? What is he trying to achieve?

Calvin had a hundred questions running through his mind, but only one of them truly mattered.

"If you aren't going to let me go, then what are you going to do with me?"

What could he want with me? I'm no use to him. He doesn't want me dead, but why does he want me alive? What can I do for him?

Felix didn't answer. He pursed his lips, checked his mirrors then changed lanes. Seemingly assured that they weren't being followed, Felix turned off the highway and into a suburban area. Calvin tensed and looked around, suspicious of an ambush or trap. They seemed to drive with no purpose, weaving deeper into the sleeping suburbs. A large tree was growing in someone's yard and Felix slowed down until they could park in front of it. The area was shadowed and not a single house had their lights on. Felix leaned into the back of the car, returning with the hard drive in his grip. He held it in his lap and stared at it with a strange reverence.

"I'm not going to leave you here to get shot," Felix said. "I'm going to try to help you."

"Help me stay alive?"

Felix shook his head. "More than that." He held up the hard drive. "I'm going to see if this can help you too."

"Help me *how*?" Calvin asked, feeling wary.

"This is my way out," Felix explained, "and now, it can be yours too. Help me. Give your own evidence. Be a witness and we'll both be out."

"What are you talking about?"

Despite his question, Calvin already had a terrible suspicion. *Witnesses...evidence...* It was all pointing in one direction.

"We have information that's priceless," Felix answered. "And now, we can trade it."

Calvin swallowed. He was right. Felix didn't want to trade the hard drive to the highest criminal bidder. He wanted to give it to someone who would use it for good—but put them in far more danger.

"You want us to be informants," he whispered.

"I already am one," Felix said. He gestured with the hard drive. "And this is my final offering. I want what I'm due...a ticket out and a new life."

Calvin's lips parted and longing filled his chest. *A new life.* It had been Calvin's fantasy for years. He wanted to be free, but he'd never been able to escape the bar. He hadn't known how to get away and had been afraid of retaliation. Now the door was thrown open. Felix was offering him the chance he'd always craved. Felix might be a far cry from his fantasy knight in shining armor, but he had a shining silver hard drive. *How much closer can I ever hope to get?* If Felix was offering to rescue him from his life at the bar and a brutal death at the hands of his old employers, Calvin would be a fool to say no.

Fresh terror flooded through him at what he was about to do, but it didn't change Calvin's decision. He was dead either way. Now, he had something to fight and stay alive for.

"Okay," he said.

Felix grinned. Calvin was struck by how handsome the guy was. He had an irresistible, cheeky smile and Calvin couldn't help giving back a small grin.

"You know," Felix said, "I never caught your name."

"Calvin."

"Well then, Calvin" — Felix pulled out his phone and flipped through the contacts — "get ready for a wild ride. We aren't free yet and we've got a lot of people who want us dead."

Calvin swallowed, his fear mixed with nausea.

"I hope that wasn't a pep talk," he mumbled.

Felix barked out a laugh as he put the phone to his ear. "I save the pep talks for the cops. They're not the ones with targets on their backs."

Calvin grimaced while Felix turned away. Felix checked the side mirrors, the rearview mirror and even looked out of the window. It seemed to take forever for the call to be answered.

"Hello, Detective," Felix said. A few seconds passed, and he chuckled before glancing at Calvin. "Funny you should mention gunshots." Felix stroked a finger over the hard drive. "I was able to get something useful." There was another pause. "Very useful. I even got you a witness."

Felix turned to Calvin again. He looked him up and down, giving Calvin a slow, thorough once-over. Calvin grew warm.

"Oh, he's a good one," Felix said, his tone bordering on flirtatious.

It's just an act. Don't you dare get flustered.

Felix had always flirted with the waitresses, never the men. He was teasing the detective, nothing more. Felix might be an attractive guy, but Calvin wasn't in the market for an informant as a boyfriend. Felix had thrown him into trouble and was offering to get him out. Calvin's only interest in the man was the hard drive and his connections to the police.

Thankfully, whatever the detective said was enough to dampen Felix's teasing.

"I got the hard drive," Felix said, his voice turning serious, "but I also got a bullet in the back windshield of my car. I need a safe space." He glanced at Calvin. "*We* need a safe space — and the protection and escape you promised me. You get the hard drive and our testimonies in exchange."

There was some talking on the other end. Calvin couldn't make it out but he could see Felix frowning in concentration. Calvin felt like a sitting duck as they waited. He started glancing out of the windows, just to make sure no one would sneak up on them.

"Damn it, Dan," Felix snapped, startling Calvin, "I don't need a police escort. I just need a goddamn place to go. Give me an address and meet us there."

There were another few moments of silence before Felix fished around in his pocket for a pen. He searched for something to write on, but when nothing was forthcoming, he reached for Calvin's hand. Calvin tried to jerk away, but Felix held on tight and started writing.

"Uh-huh...uh-huh," Felix muttered. "Yup. Done. I'll be with a redhead, taller than me with lots of freckles."

Felix hung up without letting the detective say a word. He pulled back and Calvin lost the warmth from Felix's touch. He'd been without a lover for too long, if an innocent touch was making him flush.

"Right," Felix remarked. "The place is across town, but I don't feel like driving around in such a noticeable car."

Felix put the car in gear and started driving through the suburbs. He darted his gaze over each driveway and Calvin quickly put two and two together.

"You want us to steal a car?" he demanded, feeling horrified.

"I want us to survive," Felix answered. "Dan can return the car later."

"But, Felix—"

"Ah," Felix said, his eyes bright. "That one's perfect."

Calvin followed his line of sight, finding an old sedan. It had a few dents but seemed roadworthy and well-loved. Felix circled around the block and found another quiet place to park. The suburb was sleeping in peaceful obliviousness. Felix turned off the engine and shoved his phone and the hard drive into his pocket.

"All right, let's go."

Fearful of being left behind, Calvin hurried after him. Felix was already dashing across the lawns, staying out of the direct path of any streetlights.

"Felix," Calvin whispered, running after him.

"Shh-h," Felix replied.

Felix paused, but only long enough for Calvin to catch up. He grabbed Calvin's arm then pulled him along. They ducked behind hedges and rushed across driveways as they returned to the car Felix had selected.

They had almost reached their destination when they heard the sound of an approaching vehicle. Felix jerked his head around, likely searching for cover. Calvin's heart thudded wildly as he yanked Felix backward for them to duck behind a large, trimmed bush. Felix tripped and they tumbled to the ground. Calvin hit the grass, landing on his ass with a pained grunt, Felix then falling backward on top of him. They sprawled behind the bush and quickly drew up their legs to keep out of sight. Calvin wrapped an arm around Felix to support him and hold him still. They were huddled in a half-sitting, half-lying position, and Calvin could feel Felix's heart thumping as hard as his was. It was uncomfortable and ridiculous, but the part that bothered Calvin the most was Felix's tight bottom pressing into his crotch.

The arrangement wasn't sexual, but Calvin could almost pretend it was. His face was in Felix's hair as he held the man. The hard drive was digging into Calvin's forearm and his butt still hurt from the rough landing. It wasn't perfect, but it was still the closest he'd been to another man in months. If it wasn't so damned terrifying, he could almost enjoy it.

Calvin shut his eyes and breathed in the sharp, almost-bitter cologne Felix wore. Unbidden, an image of them in this same position and naked flashed through his mind. He opened his eyes instantly, feeling foolish. He was about to be an accomplice in a car theft. There was no time for inappropriate sexual fantasies.

The car drove past them without a second glance, and Calvin breathed a sigh of relief. His eyelids did flutter closed again when Felix squirmed against him. His ass rubbed against Calvin's cock for the few seconds it took for Felix to stand. Calvin unwound his arm and looked up at the man. Felix grinned and offered him a hand, clearly oblivious to Calvin's lustful thoughts.

Calvin took it and was pulled to his feet. Felix didn't let go as they started running again. It took less than a minute to reach the driveway and their chosen car. Felix let him go and sidled up to the driver's door. He tried the door handle, but it was locked. Calvin shifted anxiously from foot to foot. He hated standing out in the open. The streetlights were bright enough to make him feel jumpy. He glanced at every window, expecting to find someone looking back. Felix didn't seem concerned. He'd left the car to search the garden beds. Calvin saw the second his gaze lighted on a large, decorative rock. Felix pulled off his jacket, revealing a dark vest over a cream dress shirt then he stepped into the garden to pick it up. After he'd wrapped it in his jacket, he came back to the car.

"Stand back," he said.

Calvin barely had time to move before Felix heaved the rock at the driver's-side window. It wasn't instantaneous and easy, like in the movies. It took considerable force to even crack the glass. Felix's jacket muffled the noise, but it was still a loud thump. Calvin darted his gaze around, fearful of discovery. Luckily, there was nothing. It took Felix two more hits before the window caved in. He cleared as much of the glass from the window frame as possible before unrolling the rock and throwing it on the ground. He put his arm inside to unlock the door and pull it open then used his crumpled jacket to brush aside the shards of glass from the seat before sitting. He leaned across and opened the passenger door.

"Get in," Felix ordered.

Calvin rushed to the passenger side then climbed in. His heart was racing, and he kept expecting someone to start shouting 'Thief!' or for neighbors to descend on them with makeshift weapons. His palms were sweating and his attention darted from the house to Felix. The man fiddled underneath the steering wheel, pulling open the console to reveal colored wires.

"We're lucky," Felix said as he worked. "I can't hotwire a modern car."

Calvin watched him nervously. Every second felt like an hour. When the engine finally turned over, Calvin let out a relieved breath and sank back into the seat. Felix pulled on his seatbelt. Calvin did the same as Felix put the car into reverse. They drove away without any sirens or shouts of alarm. *We got away with it.* Calvin let out an incredulous laugh. He rubbed his hands over his face, unable to believe it. He glanced at Felix. The man was grinning.

"First stolen car?" he asked.

"My first stolen anything," Calvin answered.

Felix chuckled. "That's a shame."

Calvin frowned. "Why?"

"Well, a first steal deserves a celebration." He offered Calvin a flirtatious wink. "Mine involved alcohol and sex."

Calvin's mouth went dry. *Stop it. He's just joking to lighten the mood.* Even if he wasn't, flirtation was a bad idea. This wasn't a thrill-seeking joyride with an attractive man. This was a mad rush to get them to safety. Calvin couldn't be distracted by a handsome face. He looked down at the writing on his hand. It was a little smudged but still readable. He used it to change the subject.

"Do you know how to get where we're going?" Calvin asked.

"Yeah," Felix answered. His focus back on the road. "It'll take about thirty minutes. Hopefully they don't find us in that time."

Calvin's stomach dropped. "Do you think they will?"

Felix shot Calvin a wary glance. "You know what happened to the last informant they found, don't you?"

Calvin's stomach roiled. "Yes," he murmured.

The stories had been graphic and widely circulated throughout the bar. No one wanted another informant getting any ideas. Calvin had tried not to listen, not because he planned to be an informant but because it only hammered home that he was trapped. Now those stories were on repeat — broken bones, blood-splattered floors and a shallow grave.

"Hey," Felix said, his voice gentling.

He even took a hand off the wheel to squeeze Calvin's shoulder. Calvin caught Felix's determined blue gaze.

"I won't let them hurt you."

Calvin scoffed. It felt like an empty promise. What could Felix do against an entire criminal organization? Why would he care about some bartender he'd never wanted at his side? Calvin turned away from him. He pressed his forehead to the window and stared out at the street. It was becoming less suburban as they headed back into the city. They'd come from the south, now they were going to the east. The address was in an older part of town with converted factories, trendy neighborhoods and numerous hotels. Calvin hoped they got there in one piece.

"What's your story?" Felix asked, breaking the quiet. Calvin shifted to look over his shoulder. Felix was watching the road, but he continued, "How'd you end up bartending at that dive?"

Calvin never spoke about his past. He didn't want to grow close to anyone and couldn't trust that what he said wouldn't be used against him. But, how much worse off could he be telling Felix?

"I ran away from home when I was sixteen," Calvin began. "I came to the big city to get away from my stepfather."

Calvin's stepfather could give some of the criminals a run for their money. His mother had married him because she'd wanted Calvin to have stability and siblings. Where his father had been kind and loving, Calvin's stepfather was heartless and cold. He hated Calvin for being a reminder of his wife's first husband. His stepfather put on a friendly front and was well-liked in the town, but behind closed doors it was a different story. His mother just couldn't see how horrible he'd been to Calvin. His stepfather was very shrewd about hiding his behavior around her. Yet, despite everything he had run away from, more than once Calvin had wished to be back there with his mother rather than alone at the bar.

"You're a lot older than sixteen," Felix pointed out.

"Yeah," Calvin admitted, shaking off the painful memories. "It's been thirteen years since I left."

Felix frowned. "You didn't spend that long at the bar. It hasn't been around that long."

"No," Calvin said. He gave a rough laugh. "No, I landed on my feet for the first ten years."

"So, what happened?"

Calvin looked back out of the window. "I met the wrong guy."

"Oh?"

Calvin closed his eyes. He hadn't talked about it in years. It didn't hurt anymore, but it depressed him to see how far he'd fallen. He'd had friends, a good job and lived in a nice part of town. All it had taken was one bad choice to bring him down.

"We got into a relationship," Calvin began. "It was fine at first, but within two years, he'd used all our money on alcohol and gambling. We lost the apartment, and when he came into my work drunk, he made a scene and punched my boss. I lost my job because of it. I had to find somewhere to go and a place to hire me — somewhere he wouldn't find me and where I wouldn't need references."

"Shit," Felix said. "That's rough."

Calvin glanced at him. Felix was still watching the road, but when he caught Calvin's gaze, his expression was compassionate. There was no pity, disgust or disinterest. It wasn't what Calvin had expected — but then, Felix hadn't been what he expected from the start — a criminal who was secretly an informant, a man who not only promised to keep Calvin safe but to share his escape ticket too. Calvin knew it wasn't wise, but he wanted to know more about him.

"What about you?" he asked. "How did you end up here?"

Felix's expression tightened. "I guess you could say it was inevitable."

"What do you mean?"

"My older brother joined a gang when we were kids. I followed along, but he was always more involved than me. I stole cars, mostly." Felix let out a sad, heavy sigh. "He died two years ago. Shot...probably by his own gang."

Calvin's breath caught. "Oh, shit."

"I haven't wanted this life for a while," Felix said. "I was content with cars when he was alive, but he always kept pushing — wanted me to climb the ladder, push drugs and earn my loyalty with a few killings." Felix clenched his jaw and shook his head. "I didn't want that."

"So, you became an informant."

Felix nodded. "I was his brother, so the cops asked me questions after he died. I didn't know anything, but I kept the detective's name in mind. I met with him a few months later and offered to get inside information to him for the right price. He agreed. Everyone in my family's dead and there's nothing tying me to the city. I had nothing to lose and everything to gain. It's been slow, but I've been carving my way out ever since."

Calvin didn't know what to say to Felix. 'I'm sorry for your loss?' 'My condolences?' or 'That must have been difficult?'. Did any of that really cover it? The last few years of Calvin's life had been hard, but he hadn't had a brother murdered or started double-crossing a criminal empire.

"That's…" Calvin struggled for words. "I'm…"

Calvin's floundering made Felix smile.

"Yeah. Talk about killing the mood."

"No," Calvin insisted, "that's not what I meant."

Felix's smile spread wider. "Don't worry about it. You can't change having a crap boyfriend, and I can't change my brother being shot."

"I feel like one outweighs the other," Calvin murmured.

Not to mention spending the last two years as a criminal informant. I've been doing it five minutes and I'm terrified.

"I don't see the point in weighing anything," Felix replied. "It sucks for both of us. What's the point in comparing?" Calvin didn't have a response to that, and before he could think of one, Felix was changing the subject. "How many years have you been at that bar?"

"Uh…three."

Felix seemed surprised. "Plenty of time to save up some coin and move on."

"To where?" Calvin countered. The reminder found frustration rushing through him, the same emotion he'd been bottling for years. "Even if I could get a better job without references, do you think they'd let me go without suspicion?"

Felix grimaced. "Right. I guess you were as stuck as I was."

They both fell silent and neither tried to start another conversation. Their talk had dredged up unpleasant memories that Calvin wanted to bury. It had also painted a picture of Felix that he wasn't sure how to accept. *I misjudged him from the minute he walked into the bar. What else have I gotten wrong?*

They drove through the city with quiet tension. It found them glancing around every street corner and into every car. Thanks to Felix's work with the rock, the window looked like it was rolled down instead of smashed. It gave them enough normalcy that no one glanced at them and their stolen car. They got through the city without incident, and it almost felt like they'd be okay. When they turned down a street two blocks from their hotel, Calvin grabbed Felix's shoulder.

"There!" Calvin gasped. "That's —"

"Pips," Felix cursed.

Pips was short and balding, but his small stature was his biggest weapon. People thought he was harmless, but he was vicious and violent. Calvin had seen him knock a man twice his size out cold in a single punch. Felix looked around before reversing the car into an alleyway. Pips was on the phone and there were three goons beside him. He was directing them to conduct a search. He hadn't noticed them yet, but if he got a look at their faces, he'd know them in an instant.

"He's checking the hotels in the area," Felix muttered.

"And he's picked the right spot," Calvin said through clenched teeth. "Ours isn't far away."

Felix already had his phone out. "I'll tell Dan and get him to send someone to shoo them away."

"Won't a police car make them more suspicious?"

"That's a risk we'll have to take."

Felix put the phone to his ear, and Calvin fidgeted in his seat, watching Pips and the others fearfully. Felix kept his voice low as he explained the situation, but Calvin's heart climbed into his throat as Pips made a gesture to his goons. They fanned out and one of them crossed the road in their direction.

"Felix," Calvin whispered, panic flooding his voice.

Felix cursed and snapped, "Now would be good, Dan."

He hung up his phone, unbuckled his seatbelt and climbed out of his seat and onto Calvin's lap. Calvin grabbed Felix's waist, gasping as the man slid their pelvises together.

"The upside of homophobia," Felix said, their faces inches apart. "Make out with a guy and they'll turn away without looking too close."

Calvin's eyes widened. "What—?"

Felix cut off Calvin's words with a kiss. He grabbed Calvin's hands and placed them on his upper back. He broke their kiss when Calvin didn't react.

"We need to appear a second away from a hand job, Calvin," he whispered. "Get into this, because your life depends on making them turn away in disgust."

Felix kissed him again, and Calvin closed his eyes. Terror was still running down his spine and he felt overly aware of how vulnerable they both were, but when Felix rolled his hips, Calvin let out a soft groan. He dug his fingers into Felix's shirt and kissed the man back.

It wasn't hard to enjoy it. Felix was attractive and kind. He'd saved Calvin's life and he was rocking their hips together. Calvin was only a man—and a single one at that. He hadn't had sex in months, and if he was going to die, why not do it making out with a handsome guy?

The danger somehow heightened the intensity. Someone could find them at any moment. They could be recognized and shot—or, if they played it right, they could be a step closer to freedom. They just needed a convincing kiss. Calvin let his body act for him. He slid his hands down to Felix's ass, tugging him forward and arching his hips. Felix let out a soft noise, but Calvin's moan was louder. He was getting hard, but he didn't care. Felix had known what he was signing up for when he'd kissed an openly gay man.

But Felix didn't flinch or stop kissing him. He slid his hands into Calvin's hair and he turned his head, brushing their tongues together. Calvin felt dizzy with desire. Felix's thighs bracketed his, making the space in the car feel overheated. He ran his hands over Felix's back and wished he could be touching skin. This was just pretend, but he might as well enjoy the myriad feelings coursing through him that he hadn't experienced in too damned long. Calvin moved back to Felix's slacks and cupped his ass. Felix's groan went straight to Calvin's cock. When Felix's growing hardness prodded his stomach, Calvin's heart leapt. *He likes this too.* Calvin wanted to get their pants open and give them both some relief. The level of his desire was rapidly approaching out-of-his control and that, along with his realization of the likely girth and length of what Felix was grinding into him, was making his mind whirl with the possibilities.

He was a second from shoving his hand between their stomachs when a tapping at the window made Calvin jump out of his skin. They broke apart and the situation flooded back around Calvin. His stomach dropped with dread, but he didn't recognize the dark-skinned man outside the window. He wasn't holding a gun. Instead, he seemed exasperated.

"If you're done almost getting shot, we should get out of here."

"If you took better care not to direct us toward the enemy, Dan," Felix fired back, "I wouldn't need a means of distraction."

"Well, bravo," Dan drawled. "You scared them away with homosexuality." Dan opened the door and made a gesture. "Now get up. We need to keep your location a secret."

Felix climbed off Calvin, pausing outside the door to lean over Calvin and grab his jacket from the driver's seat. Felix double-checked that the hard drive was still in his pocket before pulling his jacket on. Calvin couldn't help looking Felix over. His hair was a mess and his lips were swollen and pink. Calvin felt an odd mix of pride and embarrassment to find Felix was as hard as he was.

Calvin straightened his hair and tried to look less ravished as he undid his seatbelt to climb out of the car. His eyes darted over the street, but Pips and his goons were gone.

"You're the witness he told me about." Calvin turned to find the detective holding out his hand. "Detective Dan Mason."

"Calvin Hughes," he replied.

They shook before Dan directed them behind the car and down the alley.

"Is that car hot, Felix?"

"Yup," Felix said without shame.

Dan sighed, sounding weary. "We would have picked you up."

"And left us as sitting ducks? No thanks."

"You managed to be sitting ducks all on your own," Dan countered.

They met two policemen halfway down the alley. One was in plain clothes, the other in his uniform. A sense of relief flooded Calvin at seeing that uniform. It made him feel like they were finally safe. When they exited the alley at the other side, both a police car and an unmarked car were waiting for them. A female cop was standing guard and nodded at Dan. He and Felix were ushered inside the unmarked car, while Dan climbed into the driver's seat.

"When we get to the hotel, we'll do this properly, Felix."

Felix made a face. "By the book and with procedures? I like my way better…less chance of being shot."

Calvin muffled his snort. So far, Felix's way had ended up with a high chance of being shot and almost discovered. Calvin was ready for the official and, hopefully, less dangerous way. Dan shot him an amused look through the rearview mirror while Felix scowled. The expression drew attention to Felix's red and swollen lips. Calvin wet his lips and glanced away.

He willed his erection down as he looked out of the window.

They'd only kissed to stay safe and now they were with the police. There would be no reason to kiss again, and soon enough they'd be going their separate ways. A brand-new life awaited them, and Calvin would have nothing more to do with Felix. He should be counting the hours. So, why was he wondering what Felix would choose to do with his new life?

* * * *

Getting to the hotel turned out to be the easy part. The detectives snuck them in with no one the wiser, but once they were settled, the police wanted them to make statements and asked enough questions to give Calvin a headache. They interviewed them separately, made them sign paperwork and took the hard drive. The cops wanted to take them into the station in the morning, but Felix wouldn't allow it. He stood in front of Calvin, refusing to agree for them to be ferried around town, attracting attention.

Their vehemence and importance as witnesses was enough to make the detectives reluctantly agree. When they finally wrapped everything up, it was past midnight. Calvin was exhausted but remained too fearful to sleep. Police guards were stationed outside the room, but it wasn't enough to calm his shattered nerves. He feared someone would spring out of the shadows with a gun at any moment. Felix seemed unconcerned by the situation. He relaxed on the couch, playing cards. Calvin didn't know where he'd gotten the deck and was amazed that Felix could concentrate on a game. *He must have developed nerves of steel after being a secret informant for two years.*

"How are you so calm?" Calvin asked, breaking the quiet.

He could use any tips Felix would offer. He was sitting on one of the two single beds with his arms around his legs, trying not to flinch at the smallest cough from one of their guards. Dan had given them a change of clothes when they'd arrived. They were each in a white T-shirt and gray sleep pants. Calvin had showered and changed while Felix was being interviewed. Felix had only finished washing up ten minutes before. His hair was still wet.

"Panic won't get me anywhere," Felix answered. "The deal's done. It's a waiting game now." He looked Calvin up and down, frowning. "You need something to do."

Felix scooped up the cards then walked over to the bed. He took a seat in front of Calvin and began shuffling the deck. His movements were smooth and absent-minded.

"What games do you know? Gin Rummy? Blackjack? Switch?"

"I don't think I've played a card game since I was a kid."

His stepfather hadn't been keen on cards while his ex-boyfriend had liked them too much.

"Let's go with Blackjack," Felix said, beginning to deal their hands. "You've got to get as close to —"

"Twenty-one," Calvin interrupted. "Yes, I know that."

Felix chuckled as he shuffled the last of the cards. "Jacks, queens, kings are a ten and aces can be a one or an eleven." He put down the deck. "Ready?"

Calvin nodded and turned over his first cards. He ended up with a king and a jack and laughed. Felix scowled. He swept the cards away and started shuffling them again.

"Hey!" Calvin protested. "That was a good hand!"

"Beginner's luck."

Calvin rolled his eyes. "You're the one who wanted to play cards. Don't complain if you lose."

"Doesn't have to be a game. We can build a house if you like?"

Calvin shook his head, but he smiled. *How does Felix make me feel so comfortable?* His gaze traveled over Felix before stopping at the sight of the man's bare feet. It was a small thing to notice, but the fact that Felix had taken off both his shoes and socks and seemed so entirely comfortable stood out. When was the last time he'd been so casual with someone? When was the last time *Felix* had? They were dressed in pajamas, Felix's hair was still wet and they'd been making out only a few hours ago. Calvin could still remember what the man felt like pressed against him. His hands tingled and Calvin dragged his teeth over his lower lip. Felix was a good kisser. His fingers were a sight to watch as they deftly shuffled the cards. They were dexterous and long. What else would they be good at?

"Do you know how?"

Calvin blinked and jerked his focus to Felix. He felt an embarrassed flush creep up his neck. "Huh?"

"Card tricks." Felix let the cards fall from one hand to the other like a waterfall. The act was seamless and not a single card fell away. "You kept watching me shuffle."

Calvin felt his cheeks heat. He'd forgotten the cards were there.

"Uh, no. I don't know any."

Felix's smile widened, and his eyes twinkled.

"Want me to teach you?" He did the waterfall trick again. "I'm sure you'd be a natural," Felix said. "Bartending requires good hands."

Calvin swallowed. He tried not to think about getting his hands on something other than the deck. Felix had only kissed him to keep them safe. This wasn't a come-on. This was an offer for something to do and a means of distraction. He needed to get his mind out of the gutter.

"Okay," Calvin said, clearing his throat when his voice came out rough. "Teach me."

Felix grinned and shuffled up the bed. Calvin had to rearrange himself and it ended with Felix behind and leaning over him. Calvin felt each brush of their bodies. Felix didn't seem to notice Calvin's tension as he leaned close. He slid his arms around Calvin's waist and held the cards in front of Calvin for the best view.

"You want to squeeze the cards a little," Felix said, cupping them in one hand. "Let air form between them. And" — he dropped them, letting the cards fall elegantly into his palm — "they'll fall like this."

Calvin swallowed again. "Makes sense."

"Good."

Felix took Calvin's left hand and raised it into the air. He put the cards in Calvin's palm and adjusted his right hand for them to be the perfect distance apart. Calvin's skin warmed. Felix breathed softly against his neck from behind him. He smelled like soap and hotel shampoo. His hands rested warm and gentle on Calvin's wrists.

"Now, repeat what I did. Pick up the deck with your right hand. Put your thumb at the back." Calvin did as instructed, but Felix soon took Calvin's hand and rearranged it, encouraging him to squeeze the cards until they formed an arch. Felix's hand rested over his in a barely felt touch. "Hold it above your left hand."

Calvin wasn't paying attention to the words or Felix's directions. Felix was all around him and Calvin couldn't think straight. *He smells like cheap hotel toiletries. Why is that still so hot?*

"Now, let go," Felix murmured, right by his ear.

Calvin released them, but having lost focus on most of Felix's advice, it was no surprise that the cards missed his hand and some ended up halfway down the bed. When Felix laughed, Calvin shivered and his eyelids fluttered closed. It took every bit of willpower he had to stop himself from leaning back against Felix.

"Well, that could have been worse," Felix said, humor obvious in his voice.

Felix removed his arms from around him, and Calvin mourned the loss. Felix started picking up cards and Calvin did the same. He tried to use the time to clear his head, but it was hard to hold on to his determination when they adopted the same position again. Felix shuffled even closer, kneeling behind him and plastering his chest against Calvin's back, his crotch brushing the top of Calvin's ass.

"Let's try again."

Felix slid his hands down Calvin's arms, forcing Calvin to bite down on a groan. He was getting hard. *This is bad.*

"Calvin?" Felix murmured. "Are you ready?"

He turned his head to look at Felix. Their faces were inches apart. Calvin darted his gaze to Felix's lips. They'd been aroused and kissing each other only a few hours ago, and not long before that, they had been running from gunshots. Who knew what tomorrow would bring? It was worth taking a risk.

Calvin didn't second-guess. He closed the remaining space to press his lips to Felix's. It only lasted a few moments before he pulled back. He wanted more, but Calvin didn't know if Felix felt the same. Felix seemed surprised, but his shock apparently cleared and he leaned forward. Calvin let out a soft, relieved groan as Felix kissed him. Calvin dropped the cards and cupped Felix's neck. He'd been wanting this since they'd parted in the car. The man's touch was electric, and each brush of his tongue sent desire rushing through Calvin.

Felix encouraged him to lie down, even as they continued kissing, and Calvin did it eagerly. The new position found Felix straddling him, rocking their hardening cocks together. Calvin slid his fingers into Felix's hair. The damp strands were cool to the touch, and when he gently tugged on them, Felix broke the contact. Calvin surfaced from his own bliss to find that Felix was flushed and his obvious desire had blown his pupils wide.

"Well," Felix said with amusement, "I did say a stolen car deserved some sex."

Calvin grinned, but Felix stole any further response from him with another kiss. It felt good having the man on top of him, and it only got better when Felix ran his hands down Calvin's chest. Calvin arched his body closer and Felix broke the kiss with a chuckle. He trailed his mouth to Calvin's neck then sucked softly on the skin. Calvin was distracted by the nibbling. He didn't notice Felix shift off his hips until long fingers were caressing the prominent tent in Calvin's sleep pants. Calvin groaned and rolled his hips forward.

"Careful now," Felix teased. "You better not moan too loudly. We don't want our guards bursting in, thinking we're being attacked." He squeezed Calvin's cock, making him stifle a moan. "It could be awkward."

"Shut up, Felix," Calvin bit out.

Felix shifted, allowing Calvin to see his grin. He never stopped exploring Calvin's erection through the fabric.

"I'll be quiet if you will," Felix whispered, his eyes open and twinkling.

Calvin decided silence was the best response. It seemed to be the right choice. Felix let his cock go, but only so he could slip his hand inside Calvin's pants. Calvin's breath caught as Felix stroked him with his hot hand. *We should probably have some lube, but I don't want him to stop.*

Felix began with slow strokes and light squeezes just below the cockhead. Calvin was soon fully erect and leaking with arousal. Felix wiped it up with his palm and used it to help smooth his strokes. Calvin bit his lip and grunted, fighting to control his mounting desire. He arched his hips in shallow jerks. It had been far too long since he'd done this. He was flushed and sweating—and it felt amazing.

Felix leaned over him with a grin, and Calvin wanted to wipe the smugness from his face. He knew the perfect way. A wet patch was forming on Felix's pants and Calvin tugged them down to reveal his leaking, erect cock. Calvin's mouth watered, and he brought his hand to wrap around Felix's sizeable girth. Felix moaned and stopped stroking.

"Felix," Calvin whined, "don't stop."

Felix looked deeply into his eyes, but instead of resuming, he grabbed Calvin's wrist and pulled his hand away. Calvin was confused and disappointed until Felix lay down beside him on the bed. Calvin hurriedly shifted onto his side and raised his hips slightly so Felix could yank his pants the rest of the way down. They were still mostly clothed, just their hard cocks and the flushed skin of their stomachs visible. Felix brought his hand back to Calvin's cock, and Calvin took Felix's arousal in his. They both began to stroke. It took a few goes to get into a rhythm, but soon they were there and moaning.

Someone could knock on the door and step inside at any minute, but Calvin was helpless to stop his grunts of pleasure. The fear of discovery made an illicit thrill zing down his spine. It was a little dirty and very arousing, and he'd been on edge since their ruse in the alley. Calvin was desperate for release. He rolled his hips with every tantalizing touch. They had to be fast if they didn't want to be caught. The tension was coiling tighter and Calvin's muscles were like springs, just waiting to release. The stress and fear from the day needed an outlet, and Felix's grip felt so good on him. He was already on the edge and Felix seemed close too. Their breaths were coming in sharp pants and Felix's moans were becoming more frequent. Every touch was like lightning over his nerves. It was a race to the edge as they both sped up their strokes and thrusts of their hips.

"Sh-it," Felix choked, his breath hitching in the middle. "God, shit. *C-al-vi-n*."

His name was a drawn-out, lustful moan. Calvin whimpered and with two more strokes, his orgasm crashed over him. He muffled his cry by biting his bottom lip. The pleasure was overwhelming. It blanked his mind of all thought and left him boneless. It took him a few seconds to realize he'd stopped stroking Felix. The man was rolling his hips, desperate for friction, but he hadn't batted Calvin's hand away. *He wants me to get him off.* Calvin felt a rush as he tightened his grip then pumped his hand even faster. Felix's neck was arched, revealing his throat with its skin flushed pink. Calvin wanted to lick and bite it. He wanted to cover Felix' mouth with his and thrust his tongue in, working it the way he was working Felix' rock-hardness. He looked farther down. Felix's shirt was rumpled and his pants were near his knees. His toned thighs were revealed, but it was his hard, curved cock that stole the show. Calvin followed each stroke, seeing Felix's movements becoming more sporadic. Felix thrust into his palm desperately, arching his hips off the bed until he abruptly tensed. He came with a long, low groan.

Calvin watched avidly. Felix was beautiful with his head thrown back in pleasure. Calvin wanted to kiss him senseless. He wanted to see Felix come again, either with Felix's cock inside him or his inside Felix. Hell, he wanted it both ways.

But, what about the guards?

Calvin let go of Felix's cock guiltily and glanced behind him at the door. There was no startled cop staring at them. They'd been quiet enough that no one had heard.

"Well," Felix said, his voice rough and satisfied, "that was fun."

Calvin looked back at Felix. The man had shifted onto his back, seemingly spent but satiated. His eyes were half-closed.

"But," Felix continued, "I think we dirtied your bed."

Calvin glanced down, grimacing at the stains all over his blanket.

"Don't worry about it," Felix said, stretching his arms and back. He climbed off the bed, smiled and grabbed his pants. "We'll clean up and share mine. There's plenty of room."

There was no awkwardness. Felix was as relaxed and carefree as always. He even offered Calvin a hand. *How does he do that? How can he walk around with no worry or concern?* Calvin envied him that ability, even as he remained grateful for it. Felix's attitude made it easier to keep from panicking at the gunshots or feeling awkwardness at their sexual encounter. He was a rock in the sudden storm Calvin's life had become. It helped him accept Felix's offer without feeling strange as they made their way to the bathroom.

Felix wet two face towels before passing one to Calvin. They cleaned themselves and pulled their pants back on before making their way to Felix's bed. The day and the orgasm had left Calvin feeling exhausted. It kept him from worrying as he climbed beneath the sheets. Felix went around turning off lights, but when he finished, he slipped in behind him. Calvin lay on his side and Felix wrapped an arm around him, pulling him close. Felix was warm and had the strange ability to make him feel safe. They had armed police standing guard outside their room, but it was Felix's presence that allowed him to begin releasing the tension he'd held all day.

Perhaps he should have felt uncomfortable about sharing a bed with a man he barely knew and had just shared a hand job with, but Felix made it seem natural. Calvin even slipped his hand over Felix's for additional comfort. Giving a soft sigh, Calvin closed his eyes and fell asleep within minutes.

* * * *

Calvin was awakened by someone roughly shaking his shoulder. When he made a confused noise, a hand covered his mouth. He jerked, waking up faster than any coffee could manage and immediately starting to struggle.

"Shh-h," Felix said, his voice calming Calvin. "I heard a thump outside."

Felix sounded worried as he lay tense against Calvin's back. Calvin's heart raced and his palms began to sweat. Their breathing seemed too loud in the room, his fear amplifying every noise they made. With little light in the room due to the closed curtains, he could barely see that the clock read four a.m. There shouldn't have been a thump this early in the morning. When more shuffling came from the hallway, Felix removed his arms from around Calvin then climbed out of bed.

"Find something heavy," Felix whispered.

Calvin scrambled out from beneath the sheets, trying to be quiet, but his hands shook as he grabbed then unplugged the nearby clock radio. Felix slipped noiselessly into the bathroom then came back out shortly after with a can of deodorant in his hand. He paused by the bed to pick up his phone from the nightstand. His bare feet were silent as he moved to the right of the door. Shadows broke up the light from the hallway. Someone was outside their door, fiddling with the keycard lock. Felix had also secured the door with a chain, but Calvin knew it wouldn't deter the people who were after them.

Calvin held the radio against his chest, not sure what to do. Felix directed Calvin to stand behind him with his back to the wall. Calvin followed the order, trying not to make a sound. Calvin could picture Pips with a gun in hand as he waited outside, ready and willing to silence the witnesses. Calvin trembled and gripped the radio so tight that his fingers hurt.

Felix fiddled with his phone before hitting the call button. He put the phone to his ear.

"Get over here," Felix ordered, his voice barely louder than a whisper. "You're about to have two dead witnesses."

The lock beeped, and Calvin's breath left him. The door opened but caught on the chain, making their assailant grunt. Felix dropped his phone, not bothering to hang up. He placed a hand on Calvin's chest, pushing him back farther against the wall.

"Felix," Calvin whispered, bringing up a hand and gripping the man's arm.

"When they get inside," Felix murmured, "aim for their head."

"What are you going to do?" Calvin asked, panic in his voice.

Felix didn't answer. There was murmuring outside, and before Calvin could ask again, one of the intruders threw their weight against the door. The chain snapped, and the door slammed against the wall. The first man caught the wall to stay standing, while the other stormed forward.

Felix stuck out his leg, making the man stumble, but as he did, he whipped around to face Felix, who then sprayed the deodorant into his eyes. The intruder shouted in pain and brought a hand up to cover them. Felix used the distraction to kick him hard in the crotch and the guy went down. Felix dropped the deodorant and was about to punch him in the head when the other criminal caught Felix's waist and tackled him.

Calvin rushed forward and swung the radio at the head of the man holding Felix. The radio shattered and apparently caused enough pain to the guy to force him to let Felix go. Felix used the advantage to leap up then punch the criminal in the jaw and stomach.

The other man had gotten back into the action and grabbed Calvin from behind. He shouted as arms encircled his waist and arms, holding him tight. He struggled and tried to kick the guy's shins and headbutt him, but it didn't help. Calvin's panic increased when the man tried dragging him to the door. He renewed his thrashing and began to yell at the top of his lungs.

"Help! Let go of me! Call the cops! *Help!*"

"Shut up," the man spat.

Calvin ignored him and continued to fight and shout.

"Let him go," Felix demanded, having knocked his assailant unconscious.

The man removed one arm from around Calvin, but before he could pull away, the criminal pressed something small and metal to his temple. *A gun's muzzle!* Calvin went silent and froze.

"You never should have stolen from us," the man sneered.

Felix tensed, fists at his sides. His normally carefree features were hard and cold.

"Let him go. He got dragged into this. I'm the one you want, not him."

"Felix..." Calvin whispered, his heart beating wildly.

"Your bosses don't want him," Felix continued. "They want me." He took a step forward and held out his arms. "Make a trade."

Calvin sensed the criminal's uncertainty. Felix could obviously see it too, and he continued to press.

"You've lost your partner and the police will show up soon. You can't go back empty-handed. I'm the better value."

"Felix, don't!" Calvin protested, his heart pounding with fear and horror, "You know what they'll—"

"I know what they'll do to *you*," Felix interrupted, locking his eyes on Calvin's. He offered a faint smile. "I promised I'd keep you safe." He turned back to the man holding Calvin hostage. "Deal?"

"Get on your knees," the man snapped. "Hands behind your head."

Felix gritted his teeth and although he looked unhappy, he did as he'd been ordered. Calvin's heart was in his throat. Felix was defenseless. What if the man decided to shoot him? When Felix's hands were behind his head, the man wrapped his forearm arm around Calvin's throat, forcing him to tilt his head back. He couldn't see Felix. The gun left his head, and Calvin knew it was pointed at Felix.

"Where is the hard drive?"

"Let him go, and I'll tell you," Felix countered.

"You don't get to negotiate."

"I do," Felix argued. "You let him go and you get me. You stay here complaining and you get caught. *Let. Him. Go.*"

The man shifted the muzzle to Calvin's throat. Calvin gulped and shut his eyes.

"I could kill him," the criminal growled. "I could take you after he's dead."

Felix didn't respond, and Calvin squeezed his eyes shut tighter. When he swallowed, he could feel the pressure of the gun. He was more afraid than he'd ever been in his life. Calvin heard the cock of the trigger and feared he was a second from death.

"Let him go," a new male voice said.

It came from behind them, and Calvin felt a surge of hope. The criminal stiffened and didn't move, but the new voice insisted, "Do it, *now*."

Slowly, the gun left his throat, and Calvin leaped away. He spun around to see three police officers pointing their weapons at the criminal. Calvin only gave them a glance as he rushed to Felix then dropped to his knees before him, trembling. Felix's lips quirked in a grin as he searched Calvin up and down.

"Look at that," he quipped, "not even a scratch."

The remark was so flippant and ridiculous that Calvin wanted to punch the other man for not taking what had just happened seriously. But, he didn't. Instead, Calvin leaned forward and wrapped his arms around Felix, burying his face in the man's neck. Felix sucked in a startled breath, but he curled his arms around Calvin.

Calvin closed his eyes and breathed in Felix's scent. He could hear the police bustling around the room, probably handcuffing the criminals who had tried to kill them. Calvin only shifted his head when he heard someone crouch down beside them.

"Hey," the cop said, keeping his voice gentle, "let's get you two out of here."

"Somewhere safer this time?" Felix asked, a noticeable bite in his tone. "And where the hell is Dan?"

"Detective Mason is on his way," the cop said, sounding apologetic. "He lives across town."

Felix scoffed. "At least someone was fast enough to get here before they shot us." Felix ran a hand through Calvin's hair and tugged his head so their eyes could meet. "Hey," Felix said, his voice gentle. "Almost getting killed means we should celebrate—coffee, a better room and maybe some alcohol."

He winked, and Calvin barked out laugh. He was trembling and probably going into shock, but once again Felix somehow made him feel like things would be okay. He slid his hands over Felix's shirt, fisting the material. Calvin knew it was silly, but the thought of losing Felix made his heart constrict with fear.

"Don't you ever do that again," he growled.

Felix's grin spread wider and he covered Calvin's hands with his own. "I don't know. I kind of like this hero stuff."

He squeezed Calvin's fingers, and when he started to stand, Calvin grudgingly did the same. He continued to hold on to Felix as they left the room. The cop was behind them and other detectives were in the hallway. The whole area was bustling with police and curious guests, who were sticking their heads out of their rooms. They were ushered out of the hall and down to an awaiting cop car and ambulance. The paramedics rushed toward them, wanting to check them over.

"Start with him," Felix said. He flashed Calvin a comforting smile. "I'll talk to the cops."

That forced Calvin to let Felix go, despite wanting to keep him close. It felt wrong to be separated, but he had little choice. Felix sent him another reassuring grin as he stepped away. Watching him go made dark thoughts play through Calvin's mind—Felix on the floor offering his life for Calvin's. Felix being shot.

Calvin shuddered and looked away. He tried to focus on the paramedics, but it was hard. Felix had been willing to sacrifice himself. He'd fought to keep them safe and, through his efforts, they'd come out without a scratch. The man had saved his life, and all Calvin wanted was Felix's arms wrapped around him, assuring him that they were both safe and alive.

* * * *

It wasn't even eight a.m. and it was already turning into a long and horrible day. After being checked over by the paramedics, they had been taken to the station for more statements. There was an investigation being mounted into how they had been found. The criminals had knocked the guards unconscious during their shift change. It was lucky they were alive. Felix and Calvin wouldn't have fared so well if they had woken up just a few minutes later.

Calvin was sitting on an uncomfortable stool waiting for a new hotel to be arranged. The station was busy with cops walking to-and-fro and chatting in small groups. Calvin had felt jumpy for the first hour, but now, he just wanted to sleep.

He was resting his head on his palm and starting to doze off.

"Here."

Calvin jerked his head up and opened his eyes. Felix was holding out a foam cup.

"No alcohol, sadly," Felix continued. "I thought about nicking some, but figured that with all the crap we're in the middle of, I should stick to the straight and narrow."

Calvin gave him a small smile and took it. He inhaled the smell of coffee and took a sip.

The seat beside him creaked as Felix dropped down into it.

"I spoke to Dan," Felix said. "We'll be here for most of the day."

Calvin groaned. "Why? We've given our statements. What else can they possibly need?"

"Nothing, you'd think," Felix agreed. "But they wanted us here yesterday. There have to dot every I and cross every T, apparently."

"Great," Calvin muttered.

"Cheer up," Felix said, flashing him a smile. "We're unlikely to get shot surrounded by cops. We're in the safest place in the city."

Calvin looked around them. There was a police officer every few meters. The two of them were squashed in the corner while the desks of armed detectives stretched out in front of them. They *were* safe.

But Calvin couldn't help noticing something.

"They don't seem happy we're here."

It wasn't all the time, but Calvin had noticed the cops shooting them suspicious glances and disgruntled scowls.

"Nah," Felix dismissed. "That's not about you. That's all for me. They're never happy when I show up."

Calvin frowned. "But you're an informant."

"Yup," Felix said, popping the 'p'. "Doesn't change their opinion, though."

"But you're helping them take down a criminal empire. You're doing something good."

You saved my life and risked your own. You offered to share the hard drive with a stranger who needed escape just as much as you did.

Felix shook his head. "I'm saving my skin. That's all they see." He frowned. "Well, Dan sees a bit more, but he's still a cop—and I'm still a criminal." He shrugged and took a drink of his coffee. "In the end, who cares? As long as I get what I want."

And what do you want? The question was on the tip of Calvin's tongue but he swallowed it. They were stuck together by circumstance. He doubted Felix would trust him with his hopes and dreams.

"I still think they should be nicer to you," Calvin admitted. "They're nice to me, and I've been in the bar for three years."

"But you've got no record and no history of crime," Felix pointed out. "You're just a victim of crap luck."

Calvin didn't like the unfairness of it. He'd done nothing to help stop the criminals. Felix had put his neck on the line for years. *How am I the one they like more? I'm here by nothing but accident.* But before he could say anything, a cop was walking up to them.

"White, get your ass up. Detective Mason wants to speak to you."

Felix plastered on a bright smile. "That's my cue." He winked at Calvin. "I'll try and pilfer some donuts on my return."

The cop's expression turned sour, but Felix didn't let it bother him as he walked through the station with his head held high. Calvin watched him with admiration. Felix seemingly didn't let anything destroy his good mood or waver him from his path—not criminals, cops or even the loss of his brother.

Felix White. Maybe he's more like a knight in shining armor than I thought? Calvin smiled into his next sip of coffee. And when Felix returned nearly an hour later, he had the promised donuts, along with more caffeine. Calvin was called in a few minutes later to give a detailed account of his time at the bar. He only saw Felix in passing for the next few hours.

When late afternoon came and they had a place to go, Calvin was grateful to leave the station. Even though he'd felt safe surrounded by cops, there was a menacing energy in the air there, like all hell could break loose right on his head at any minute. At least outside the station he could breathe a little more freely.

The detectives took them to the police garage then shuffled them between three different cars to avoid detection. The police weren't taking any chances as they relocated them to a more upmarket hotel, which was decadent and better protected. Everything was going fine and Calvin was feeling happy with the new arrangements until they were given separate rooms. Calvin watched from the hallway as Felix was led to a room four doors down. Calvin's escort opened his door and examined his room from top to bottom before deeming it 'safe'. He then gave the key to Calvin and told him a cop would stay in an adjoining room. The man then left Calvin alone.

Calvin stood in the center of the room feeling lonely and uncomfortable. The curtains were open, filling the room with light. Calvin needed it. It kept the shadows at bay, just like Felix did. He hadn't felt fear for hours because Felix's words had made him feel safe. *We're unlikely to get shot surrounded by cops. Safest place in the city.* Now, he was alone in a hotel room. He'd almost been kidnapped from a room similar to this. The only thing to save him was Felix. He wanted the man back.

Pull yourself together. You barely know him. You don't need his company to be protected.

Calvin gritted his teeth and tried to shake it off. He wasn't normally so dependent on another person. He'd managed fine on his own for years. He didn't need Felix. He didn't need anyone.

Feeling frustrated, Calvin yanked off his shirt and headed into the bathroom. The shower was hot and had excellent pressure. It helped calm him down and loosen the tension in his muscles. He did remain jumpy, unable to close his eyes without fearing someone would burst in at any moment.

When he stepped back into the room, he half expected Felix to be there playing cards — but he wasn't. Calvin sighed and dropped his towel. He had new clothes to change into and he pulled them on with his mind on Felix. *What is he doing? Is he thinking about me?*

"Damn it," he cursed, throwing his towel into the bathroom.

He might not need Felix, but it didn't mean Calvin didn't miss him. Sitting on the bed with his face in his hands, Calvin wished Felix were there. He wanted to see Felix's cheeky smile and be distracted by the man's stories or card games. Maybe they could even be intimate again, if he was lucky.

When a knock came at the door, Calvin jerked his head up in surprise and with a bolt of fear.

"Calvin," Felix called, "don't have a panic attack."

That made Calvin smile. His heart began to slow and he stood with relief then hurried to the door. He checked the peephole, just in case, but it was only Felix. He unchained and opened it. Felix was barefoot and in a fresh change of clothes, too. His hair was wet again, just like the previous night and Calvin itched to run his fingers through it as he had before.

"What are you doing here?"

Felix shrugged. "I don't like my room."

"And you want mine?"

Felix smiled. "Yours does seem nicer." He didn't even look at the room. He held Calvin's gaze. "Want to share?"

Any remaining worry Calvin had dissolved in that moment. He nodded and, in response, Felix stepped closer. Calvin welcomed him. He cupped the man's neck and slid his fingers into Felix's hair. Felix brought his hands to Calvin's waist and their lips came together. It wasn't a deep kiss. Instead, it was almost reaffirming.

We're both okay. We're both alive.

When they pulled apart, they just stared at each other. So much had happened, and so much had changed. Felix had gone from being just another criminal in the bar to someone Calvin would trust with his life.

"It's been a long day," Felix said, stroking his hips. "We could use some rest."

The idea of climbing into bed with Felix at his side was the nicest thing he'd been offered all day.

"That sounds perfect."

Felix grinned. They pulled apart, but only so Felix could step inside. Calvin shut then locked the door. When he turned around, Felix kissed him. Calvin melted into the embrace. He wrapped his arms around Felix's waist and enjoyed the slow brush of their mouths. But Felix wasn't content with a chaste kiss. He slid his hands over Calvin's sides in a teasing hint of what he had in mind. Calvin moaned and pulled back.

"I thought you said we needed rest?" Calvin questioned, despite his growing interest.

"I like to go to bed on a high note," Felix replied with a grin.

Calvin licked his lips. "Does your guard know you're here?"

"Yeah," Felix said. "I told him if he didn't want to see us with our pants down to leave us alone for an hour or so."

"*Felix*," Calvin groaned, trying to muster embarrassment but ending up amused. "They're supposed to be protecting us."

"And they will. But it's better for everyone if they don't run in at the first cry one of us makes. Don't you agree?"

Calvin's blush finally heated his cheeks, but when Felix kissed him again, Calvin stopped thinking about the cops. He slipped his hands under Felix's shirt, only to feel Felix tug him farther into the room.

Calvin broke the kiss to make sure they wouldn't trip, yet he was distracted from looking around them. His gaze was locked on Felix. The cheeky smile he'd missed was curving Felix's lips and his eyes sparkled with humor and desire.

Felix took his hands and stroked his thumbs over Calvin's palms. He looked thoughtful.

"I noticed you at the bar, you know."

"You did?"

"Yeah. I've always been partial to men who were good with their hands."

Calvin was surprised. "You always flirted with the waitresses."

"And you *didn't* flirt with the guys." Felix shrugged. "I didn't want to get noticed. You probably didn't either."

"No," Calvin agreed. "I kept my head down."

"Until I crashed into you," Felix said, following it with a chuckle.

Until you gave me the freedom I've always wanted.

He couldn't thank Felix enough for everything he'd done, but Felix wasn't seeking gratitude. His interest was obviously more base. They'd reached the bed and Felix let his hands go to curl two fingers in the band of Calvin's pants.

"We should tell Dan to get us some better clothes."

"I don't think we're meant to be leaving the hotel, so it doesn't matter."

"True." Felix caught his gaze. "And that gives me more chances to teach you card tricks."

Calvin laughed, but the sound was smothered by Felix's lips. Calvin's eyes fell closed and he forgot about anything that wasn't Felix.

Calvin ran his hands over Felix's chest and hips, shivering when Felix responded in kind. They hadn't had the chance to explore each other yesterday. Now, Calvin could touch at his leisure. Felix's body was warm and firm under Calvin's hands while his lover was using slow and curious fingers to circle his nipples. They never stopped kissing. Every brush of Felix's tongue against his sent lust flooding Calvin's body and hardening his cock.

Calvin didn't know what he wanted to do first.

He started with running his hands back under Felix's shirt. He'd never managed to see Felix naked the last time. *That needs to change.* Calvin started pulling on the garment. Their kiss broke and Calvin got the shirt over Felix's shoulders and onto the floor. His lover's chest was finally on display. Calvin traced a scar under Felix's right collarbone.

"I tried to unlock a door through a broken window," Felix explained. "I was sixteen and stupid."

Calvin smiled faintly. "Car window?"

"A house, actually. I stuck to stealing cars after that."

The absent comment highlighted how little he knew about Felix.

What other scars does he have? What crimes has he taken part in? What does he want to do with his new life?

Calvin found the only question he cared about learning was the last one. But his intrigue wasn't enough to have him stop what they were doing. There would be plenty of time for asking his questions later.

Felix caught Calvin's shirt and quickly pulled it off. The freckles on Calvin's face extended all over his body and Felix grinned, thumbing a patch of them.

"So many to kiss. Too bad we only have an hour."

Calvin swallowed. "Planning on going somewhere?"

"Nah. Told you... Your room is nicer. But I'd rather not give the cops an eyeful."

Felix slipped his hand to Calvin's hip before palming his ass. Calvin's cock was already half-hard and Felix was only encouraging his erection.

"Then we'd better hurry up," Calvin said a little breathlessly.

He grabbed Felix's pants and slipped his fingers underneath the waistband. His mouth went dry when he realized the man wasn't wearing any underwear. He gripped Felix's shaft, making his lover give a grunt of pleasure before tipping back his head. Calvin stroked

Felix's cock, feeling it stiffen further under his touch until it reached full arousal.

"Damn," Felix gasped. "You really are good with your hands."

"I'll be even better if your pants come off."

Felix chuckled. "Then let me fix that."

He began to step away and Calvin removed his hand. Felix shoved off his pants and climbed onto the bed. He crooked his finger for Calvin to join him. After stripping off his own clothes, he knelt in front of Felix on the mattress.

Felix grasped Calvin's cock and he groaned and jerked his hips. Felix gently stroked him, working his cock until he was stiff and aching.

"Forget asking for clothes," Felix muttered. "I'm asking Dan to get us some condoms and lube."

Calvin laughed, but his amusement mixed with anticipation. While he would have loved something more tonight, he wouldn't complain about what he did have. It wasn't the perfect situation, but it was more than he'd expected, and even if it wasn't exactly his dream-come-true, it sure was nice — not to mention that the promise of sleeping with Felix in the future was something to look forward to. *If he mentioned getting condoms and lube, then he must want that too.*

Pressing forward, Calvin kissed his lover. Felix made a small noise of surprise, but kissed back. Calvin kept moving until Felix was on his back and Calvin was leaning over him. Felix's hand had loosened, but Calvin slipped his between their bodies to grasp Felix's shaft.

Felix moaned into his mouth. He gripped Calvin again and the kiss broke as Calvin gasped. His opened his eyes and caught Felix's gaze. The man's pupils were blown with lust and his lips were red from their kisses.

"Didn't peg you for a top," Felix teased, "but it seems fair. I got you into this mess. Now, you call the shots."

Calvin could make a joke, but he didn't want to. He'd never expressed his gratitude, and now was his opportunity.

"Top…bottom, doesn't matter, but from where I'm sitting," Calvin replied, "it wasn't a mess. It was exactly where I've always wanted to be."

Felix either didn't notice or ignored the severity of the moment. His eyes were dancing with humor as he asked, "Between my legs?"

Calvin rolled his eyes, not feeling surprised.

"You never take *anything*, seriously."

"Your hand is on my cock. I'd rather we only take things *sexually*."

Calvin snorted, but before he could reply, Felix softly touched his arm. Calvin had looked away but he met Felix's gaze again. The amusement that had shown in his eyes had been replaced by a gentle understanding. Calvin didn't need any further conversation to know his words had been acknowledged, and the warm feeling it gave him was one he hadn't experienced in quite some time, if ever.

Calvin kissed Felix once more and returned his attention to Felix' erection. He was happy to continue now that Felix knew the truth. He started to pump Felix's cock, making his lover suck in a breath before matching his rhythm. They didn't maintain their kiss, breaking apart to pant. Calvin brushed his lips over Felix's jaw while Felix slid his other hand over Calvin's back and drew him closer. Calvin bowed his head and it gave him a perfect view of Felix's chest and his thick, white scar. Calvin wanted to trace it with his tongue, but he settled for squeezing Felix's cock and increasing his speed. Felix's hips jerked but he was quick to respond in kind, making Calvin rock forward.

He wasn't as fueled by adrenaline or fear as he had been the previous night, but his body was still aching for an orgasm.

"Felix," he gasped.

Felix increased his motions and Calvin did the same. Their hands were a blur. Felix tipped back his head, exposing his throat and Calvin arched his spine.

"Come on," Felix panted. "Come on."

Calvin didn't know if Felix was urging him to climax or to speed up his strokes, but the man's skin was flushed and his breathing was heavy. He looked close, and so was Calvin. Felix was as talented with his hand on a cock as it was with cards. Calvin's arousal was heavy and throbbing. It wouldn't take long to make him climax.

"Felix," he groaned.

He jacked the man's cock and squeezed the shaft before twisting his wrist, holding it below the head. Felix stiffened and, with a hitched cry, he came. Calvin was surprised. He glanced up and took in Felix's parted lips and blissed expression. The sight shot heat through his body and made his erection pulse with need of release.

Calvin let go of Felix's cock and grasped his lover's lax hand to encourage Felix to stroke him again. Felix quickly complied and with two more strokes, Calvin's orgasm overtook him.

Calvin caught his breath as he recovered, feeling wrung out and exhausted. It made him remember how little he'd slept.

When Felix abruptly laughed, Calvin opened his eyes.

"This time, we didn't ruin the bed," he said, grinning. "Just me."

Calvin glanced down at the mess and winced. He climbed off Felix and said, "Give me a second."

He hurried into the bathroom and wet a towel. He cleaned his hand and the little of his thighs that needed it before bringing the cloth to Felix, who swiftly cleaned himself. When he was done, Felix left the bed for the bathroom.

In his absence, Calvin admired the bedspread. They'd rumpled it, but Felix was right. There was no other indication of their activities. When Felix returned without the towel, he ignored his clothes to drop back onto the mattress. So simple, so easy, so *Felix*. He slipped under the sheets before holding them up in open invitation. Calvin smiled and joined him. He put his back to the man and Felix brought his arm around Calvin's waist, just like they had done it the last time. Looking down at Felix's arm, it suddenly reminded him of what he'd almost lost. *If the cops had been only a few minutes later…*

The memory made fear catch in his throat, and before Calvin could second-guess, he was speaking. "Would you really have given yourself up for me?" he asked.

Felix was silent so long that Calvin didn't think he was going to answer.

"Yeah," he eventually admitted, "I would have."

Calvin swallowed and took Felix's hand, gripping it tightly. "I don't want you to do that."

"I don't want to either," Felix said quietly. He shifted and let their fingers link. "So," he continued, his voice upbeat and teasing again, "the cops better get more efficient at their jobs. I need my beauty sleep."

Calvin shook his head with exasperation. "Will you *ever* take something seriously?"

"Nah. It's a waste of time." He shifted, moving even closer. He brushed his lips along the back of Calvin's neck. "Better things to focus on."

Calvin stiffened, but Felix continued to press soft kisses against his skin. When Felix stopped, Calvin held his breath, not sure what to expect.

"What do you want from your deal?" Felix asked. "What do you want the cops to give you?"

Calvin suddenly felt nervous. He'd been wondering about Felix's motivations for hours and now he was the one who was pressed for an answer.

Will it seem silly to him?

"A new life," he answered truthfully. "A small house, a simple job. Just...a normal life."

Felix gave a soft sigh against his skin.

"Funny, you say that," he murmured. "It's what I want too." Calvin sucked in a breath, but Felix hadn't finished. "We've got a while before the trial, Calvin. We'll be stuck in this hotel, waiting for our escape. It might be lonely, staying in separate rooms all on our own. Maybe we should stay together?"

Calvin's body flushed with warmth and excitement. They had weeks, maybe even months of hiding before their case could come to court. They could get to know each other and explore each other's bodies and personalities. It was a chance to see if the connection and tension between them was adrenaline-based or something far more special. Calvin didn't have to think twice.

"I'd like that," he admitted.

"I'll tell Dan to cancel the other room tomorrow," Felix said with a grin. He pressed another kiss to Calvin's shoulder, followed by his neck. "I'm too busy tonight."

Felix could just have meant sleeping, but Calvin was still delighted by all the possibilities that suddenly now existed for him, for them. They had the night to themselves and Calvin couldn't wait to see what it and the future would hold.

There was still danger around the corner and no guarantee that they would remain safe, even after the trial was over, but Calvin felt hopeful. He also believed that his best fantasies and deepest wishes were beginning to come true. Felix wasn't a conventional knight-in-shining-armor, but if they could still ride off into the sunset for their 'happily ever after', then that was all Calvin needed. *Love* was all he needed.

Who needs a blond dream man who helps old ladies across the street? I have Felix White, and he beats any fairytale.

Want to see more from like this?
Here's a taster for you to enjoy!

Brothers in Arms
Megan Slayer, Helena Maeve, Lucy Felthouse, Anna Lee and Thom Collins

Excerpt

Excerpt from One Night with You

I need a night to remember and forget. Tate Gibson sat in his car in the parking lot of Donovan Apartments and stared at the building. Although he saw the shadows moving in front of the windows, he wasn't paying any attention. He had too much on his mind. He hadn't planned on making the detour home and sure as hell not for the reasons he'd come back to where he'd grown up.

He drummed his fingers on the steering wheel. His friend Blake had sworn the party would be a good way to get his mind off his troubles. He had to be crazy. Coming to the college for a night of drinking and possibly hooking up with someone wouldn't take his mind off anything. Still, he hadn't driven across town to sit in his car.

Tate left the vehicle and hit the lock. In less than forty-eight hours' time, he'd be on his way back to South Korea. He scrubbed the top of his head with his palm. Jesus. He'd been through too much in the last year. He didn't mind coming home, but not for a funeral. He was too young to deal with this kind of heavy psychological stuff.

"Get your ass in here," Blake shouted out of his front window. "Been waiting for you."

He sighed. Trust Blake to know when he needed to be pulled out of his own head. He strode across the parking lot to the apartment building. Someone had propped the door open and people milled around the foyer as well as up the stairs to the second level. He snorted as he approached the door to Blake's. A thick rock held the door open and music blasted into the hall.

Blake appeared in the doorway and held a plastic cup. "About damn time."

"It's not a good day, okay?" He stuffed his hands into his jeans pockets. "Lay off."

"I've got someone here I want you to meet." Blake draped his arm around Tate's shoulders and steered him into the apartment. "He's sweet and handsome and loves to suck cock."

Finding a fuck friend for the night appealed to Tate, but he disliked when Blake set him up. "I don't know." Blake's taste in men left more than a little to be desired.

"Bullshit. You do, too. You want someone to make you forget, right? Even if for an hour? He'll hit the spot." Blake marched Tate up to a man with blond hair and a tattoo on the side of his neck. The man grinned and folded his arms. The muscles in his upper body bulged.

"This is Lance. He's up for anything and clean." Blake pushed Tate into Lance. "You're welcome."

Tate eased back a foot and forced a smile. He didn't mind tats on anyone, but the neck tat of a skull breathing fire turned him off.

"So, I hear you're in the Army." Lance nodded. "You're a runner, too?"

Oh fuck. "Yes, on the runner part. It's how I blow off steam, but no on the Army part. I'm in the Air Force. I oversee maintenance on the planes and work on them when they break down or are damaged."

"Uh-huh." Lance's eyes widened. "Sounds exciting." He sipped from his plastic cup. "Uh, do you want a beer?"

"Sure." Truth be told, he didn't need the alcohol, but he doubted Lance would keep up the conversation without it. He drifted to the edge of the living room and surveyed the crowd. For only twenty-six, he felt a lifetime older than the rest of the people at the party. Most of the men and women were still in college, worrying about papers, exams and life beyond graduation. Not him.

He'd spent the last two days talking his mother down from her emotional ledge and suppressing his own feelings. He shook his head. He didn't belong there. He'd been given five days' leave and should be at home. Christ, there was so much to do. He refused to let anyone down again. What did he think he'd accomplish by going to a party? He could hear his sister's voice in his head, reminding him to have fun. Fat lot of good that did for her. He'd gone off to join the Air Force and left her behind. She'd told him she'd be all right. Promised him she'd stay out of trouble. He should've known from the first moment he'd seen her latest boyfriend, Aaron, she'd be in for a world of hurt. He hadn't held up his end of the deal. He'd let her live her life and in return, she ended up dead. His mother blamed him and Aaron, despite being the reason she'd gotten into the damn car, swore Tate's leaving had caused her to act recklessly. Fucking hell. He so did not belong at a party.

Tate kept his hands in his pockets and strode across the room. At the doorway, he collided with a solid body. "Sorry," he muttered. When he glanced up, he stared into the bluest eyes he'd ever seen. "Whoa."

The owner of the blue eyes grinned. "Hi."

"I'll get out of the way. I was just leaving." Tate ducked into the hallway and the cooler air.

"Are you okay?" the man said. "You look lost. Did someone slip you something? I told Blake not to have that shit here."

Excerpt from Spoil of War

The sky was an iridescent crimson, streaked with the white contrails of seven frigates slowly closing on Rune Station. Forty-eight days ago, there had been three times that number. Without the ceasefire, there would have been far fewer.

Relief at the sight of the battered Valiant overrode Briar's distaste for the armistice. His heart pounding with a mixture of anticipation and apprehension, he fought the urge to rush ahead of his fellow officers. There were only a dozen of them, far fewer than the hundreds of civilians gathered to welcome back their loved ones, and none of his peers were given over to displays of sentiment.

Flexing his hands behind his back, Briar blinked back the moisture in his eyes.

One after the other, the massive hatch doors of the ships hissed open, disgorging blue uniforms, then gray, then the familiar black of the Expeditionary Forces, more colloquially known as the Executioners.

Murmurs rippled over the crowd, cresting into shouts of bewilderment and consternation.

Not all of the men and women exiting the frigates did so on their own two feet. Steel boxes draped in the Federation flag gleamed under the dull morning sun.

Suddenly, the mob rushed the barricades, leaving the infantry guardsmen torn between repelling what was beginning to look like an insurgency and treating inviolable military families as though they were cattle.

A familiar pair of shoulders stretching a black jumpsuit distracted Briar from the budding fracas. Could it be? The procession thinned gradually to reveal the silhouette in its entirety, all six feet two of it mercifully stalking down the landing strip unaided, head down, hair a little longer than Briar had last seen it. His fingers itched to knot in those reddish strands. His chest ached even as the weight upon his heart lifted.

All around him, men and women wept and kissed and embraced, their voices like so much white noise, and yet he stood there, frozen, waiting for Kai to glance up.

Briar knew the precise moment when he was recognized. Kai's whole frame loosened, his full lips almost twitching into a small smile. Then, shadow, his features darkening. Briar's first thought was that Kai had been wounded, that something was wrong. He even thought he might be hallucinating. But no, that was very much his partner marching toward him, his broad strides now slightly less purposeful. It took him a long beat to register the silver lead in Kai's hand, tethering him to the bound wrists of the prisoner beside him.

In the forty-eight days since Kai had left, Briar had imagined and reimagined what he would say when they were reunited. At no point did he expect to begin with, "What have you done?"

He also didn't expect Kai to look to the handsome stranger on his right and say, "Briar, meet Dallan. He's—"

"Yours."

Between those dark eyes and dimpled cheeks, even a saint would've forgotten himself with the man— never mind a lonely captain in a high-stress environment.

"Ours," Kai corrected, though it was visibly a technicality.

The cacophony of sobbing and laughter echoing all around them finally pierced Briar's bubble. "I see," he said, making himself nod. "The cog's this way."

He turned away before Kai could see him grimacing, the pressure on his chest well and truly restored.

Excerpt from Would You Wait for Me

As he kissed along Lucas's jaw, Kip wished they could stay here in this moment. Freeze time. He didn't want to leave his lover. But his duffel was by the door and in the morning he'd drive back to the base and be deployed to Iraq.

Lucas pulled him in for a kiss. "Stay with me, babe."

"I want to," Kip whispered, gazing at him. He knew Lucas meant in the here and now but he voiced his thoughts. He braced his hands on either side of Lucas's head. Their naked bodies entwined with the twisted sheets. They were both still half-hard even though they'd just made love.

"I know." Lucas's sea-blue eyes teared up. "Promise me something?"

"Anything."

"Come home to me. Make it through this tour and get back here. I don't... I can't lose you."

He moved and wrapped Lucas in a hug. "You won't." He brushed his lips to Lucas's forehead, pushing back his brown curls. "Promise me you'll wait for me?" He wanted to be everything Lucas needed. And he hoped his promise would be enough.

"I will," Lucas swore, giving him a small smile.

"Then I'll do anything I have to so I can get back here to you." Kip kissed him softly, but the kiss became fueled by need and the desire to not part. He rolled Lucas over so he was on top once again, their cocks languidly sliding together. "I love you, Luc."

"I love you, too." Lucas clung tightly to him as they rocked toward their climaxes. They reached it together, falling into pleasure as they held onto one another. Kip wanted to sear this into his memory — this would be a moment he'd remember to get him through the rough and lonely days ahead.

* * * *

The next morning came way too soon. Kip showered and dressed as Lucas ordered them breakfast. They shared pancakes and coffee on the unmade bed. As they ate, Kip wondered when they'd be together again. He had his orders, but he could return sooner or even later. Eight months was a long time. They could write letters, sure, but phone calls would be few and far between to avoid suspicion. And Skyping was out. Any rumors could get back to his father, the base commander, and he'd be forced to come out. He wasn't ready for that yet. He wanted to openly declare he was in a relationship with the beautiful man beside him, but he was afraid of the risks. There were so many to think about where he was going. He sighed and Lucas looked up from his cup. "What is it?"

He reached over to caress Lucas's cheek. "Nothing. You know we'll have to celebrate our anniversary when I get back." Four years ago, when Jax—Kip's German Shepherd—had fallen ill, they'd met while Lucas had been doing an internship. They'd just clicked and Lucas had been a good friend when he'd made the difficult decision to put the dog to sleep as he'd had a brain tumor. Friendship had slowly become more, and Lucas had agreed to keep their relationship a secret during his first tour. Since then, they'd fallen in love, but were still hiding it from everyone. And here he was, ready for the next deployment.

"Four years next month." Lucas smiled. Then he ran a hand through his hair. "I wish I could go with you right now. See you off."

"I know, but it's better this way. We can say our goodbyes and I can kiss you all I want."

Lucas leaned over and gave him a coffee-flavored kiss. "Promise you'll at least think about me being at the homecoming when you get back?"

"I will." Kip gazed at him. "I'm really going to miss you."

"Me too." Lucas bit his lip. "I'm going to start interviews next week. I'm hoping if I can get a decent job I could get a bigger place. Then we wouldn't have to come here all the time."

Kip was staying in the barracks, and they could barely turn around in Lucas's apartment, so the hotel was a nice place for them both to get away from it all. "Didn't Brianna say she'd have a spot for you once you got your degree?"

"She did." Lucas nodded. "And my aunt might be moving to Florida, so there's another option."

"Oh, yeah? She'll give you the house?"

"Not outright, but it could be mine… Ours," he said quietly.

"That would be great… I gotta go, baby. We'll talk about this more later, okay?" Kip grabbed his duffel and cap. He checked the clock. "I'm already pushing it."

"I'll hold you to that." Lucas jumped up and walked over to him. He adjusted Kip's jacket, then cupped his face and kissed him so softly it took Kip's breath away.

He put Lucas's hand on his heart. "I'm leaving this here, keep it safe."

There were tears in Lucas's eyes and he just nodded. For a moment he was silent, then he said, "I'll write you every day."

"And I'll call when I can." Kip embraced his lover and breathed him in. It took every ounce of willpower to step away and go to the door. "I'll be back before you know it."

"You'd better be." Lucas gave him a watery smile. "Love you, Kip."

He turned back and grinned at Lucas, putting on a brave front and feigning confidence he didn't feel. "Love you, Lucas." He hefted his bag over his shoulder and walked away, already wishing he didn't have to leave.

Excerpt from An Interesting Find

Closing his book with a very final slap, Nathan then put it on the coffee table in front of him. He leaned back in his chair. Stretching languidly, he said, "Bloody good, that was. Though, admittedly, I thought it'd last me all week. Wasn't expecting to get through it on day one."

Raising an eyebrow, Lee shot Nathan an amused glance. "Not far off myself. Fucking storm. Stupid us, eh, going on holiday in the UK in summertime—not like you can guarantee the sodding weather, is it? Should've gone to the Canaries."

"No, we can't guarantee the weather, but…" Nathan gave the window a sidelong glance, "I do have some good news."

"Yeah?"

"Yeah. The torrential downpour has stopped."

"Seriously?" Lee slammed his own book closed and scurried over to the window. "Oh, wow, it's cleared right up, and I can see a rainbow. Wanna head out? Just a little wander down to that pond we saw on the way here, maybe? Get some fresh air. We've got loads of daylight left, haven't we?"

Nathan checked his watch. "Yeah, plenty. Especially if we're only nipping to the pond. It's probably only a fifteen-minute walk."

"Fantastic. I was going a bit fucking stir crazy in here. I'll grab our coats and shoes."

Lee had disappeared into the hallway of their rented holiday cottage before Nathan had the chance to reply. Shaking his head with a smile, Nathan collected their empty mugs from the coffee table and took them into the kitchen, then got a bottle of water from the fridge. He doubted they'd need a drink during their short trek along the road, but he could just shove the bottle in his coat pocket and forget about it. At least it'd be there if they wanted it.

When he returned to the living room, Lee was just about to tie up his laces.

"I got water," Nathan said, brandishing the bottle.

"Cool. Shoes are there." He nodded to the chair Nathan had been sitting in. Sure enough, his trail shoes were waiting on the floor in front of it.

"Thanks."

Within a few minutes, they were headed out of the door. Nathan locked up, pocketed the key, then checked the handle. He doubted very much the place would get broken into — they were in the middle of nowhere, after all. There were farms nearby, but the closest village was about a mile and a half away. So any thieves would have to make a considerable effort to get to the cottage in the first place, never mind attempt to break into it. Rolling his eyes at his own paranoia, he turned and followed Lee, who'd already started walking slowly along the road in the direction of the pond.

After falling into step beside Lee, Nathan pulled in some deep breaths, enjoying the fresh air after being cooped up in the cottage. It was a beautiful and cozy place, but it was supposed to be a base for them to go walking — somewhere for them to eat, sleep and shower, not to be stuck in for hours on end, staring at the walls. Or climbing them.

He admired the rainbow as they walked, its vivid colors painted across the watery sky. It seemed the clouds had literally exhausted themselves — only occasional wispy streaks of white now interrupted the never-ending blue. The sun beamed down, heating up the ground and beginning to evaporate the huge puddles. It would take some doing — one such puddle stretched across the width of the road, and they had to skirt around its edge to avoid getting wet feet.

Nathan smiled. Though the storm itself had been grim, the washed-out aftermath made everything feel fresh, clean somehow.

"You look thoughtful," Lee said, breaking into his reverie. "A penny for them?"

"Mmm. It's one of those things that sounds better in your head than said out loud."

"Try me."

Shrugging, Nathan replied, "Nothing major. Just admiring the rainbow, the sky, the clouds... Thinking how everything looks so fresh and clean after a good storm. Like it's been purified or something... Ugh, it's stupid."

Lee stopped and reached for Nathan's hand. His green eyes were wide and filled with wonder. "No, it isn't. Not at all—I was thinking something similar myself. It's kinda romantic, isn't it? Purification, rebirth, and all that."

"In a roundabout way, maybe. I dunno." He shrugged again.

Lee's eyes narrowed, and his lips curved into a wicked grin. "We could make it romantic."

"How so?"

"Come here and I'll show you." Still gripping Nathan's hand, Lee tugged him close and moved in for a kiss. Nathan went into the embrace willingly, the smile on his face soon smothered by Lee's hot lips.

Twining their arms around each other, they deepened their kiss. Mouths opening, tongues searching, stubble scratching. Nathan moaned, tucking his hands under the back of Lee's waterproof coat and gripping his firm, muscular arse cheeks. Arse cheeks he'd parted a thousand times, exploring between them with fingers, tongue, cock...

His head swum with erotic images, and he suddenly wished more than anything that they were back at the cottage so they could take things further. Oh, the irony — they'd been in the place all bloody day, eager to leave, and now they'd left, he wanted to return.

Reluctantly, he broke the kiss. "Phew." He blinked rapidly, trying to reclaim his equilibrium. Blood and adrenaline rushed around his body, making him a little unsteady. "That was…intense."

"And romantic." Lee grinned, the mischief and arousal in his eyes blatant.

Excerpt from Gods of Vengeance

It rained the day they buried Owen Hazard at the church on Hammerscliffe Peak. None too heavy — just a misty drizzle to match the muted sky and the gray spirits of the mourners who gathered at the church and, later, the graveyard. They laid Owen to rest in the grave beside his grandparents. It was a family plot, and many tears were shed at the sight of his coffin going into it too soon. He was only thirty-three.

Riley Brook held his own tears in check. He had cried enough already — all of this last week. Let the others weep. They needed it now — he didn't. His pain and grief had been replaced by colder, far harder emotions — anger and the unremitting need for revenge. The cold rain ran down his forehead, over his narrow brow and into his eyes. He didn't blink it away, didn't flinch as it dripped from the tip of his long, straight nose. He felt it on his neck and down the collar of his white funeral shirt, but it didn't bother him. That kind of discomfort was irrelevant now.

The turn-out for the funeral was immense. The farming community came out en masse to honor their dead. Especially the loss of someone so young. A son, a husband and a father — the tragedy of Owen's death touched every person in that ancient churchyard.

Somber-faced men in long overcoats held the hands of wives and girlfriends, unified by the senselessness—a life over too soon.

Owen's wife, Susan, mother of his three children, just about kept it together. Sandwiched between Owen's sister, Julie, and Pam, her best friend from the village, her features were a transparent mask of suffering. Riley had never seen grief etched so large on a human face. His mother and father stood close by in bewildered misery—it was every parent's greatest fear, to see their children buried.

Next to them stood a man who Riley had not seen in almost ten years. Mark Hazard, Captain Mark Hazard, Owen's older brother. Though he was undoubtedly handsome, Mark's face was devoid of any emotion. He stood rigid with his shoulders back and spine straight, as if he was on the deck of his ship, ready for inspection. Mark had changed little in all those years. The lean jaw, wide mouth and neat brown hair were just as Riley remembered. Mark looked stronger now. Broader. There were lines around his eyes but they suited him. He'd grown more handsome with age.

Mark had been posted in the Eastern Mediterranean when his brother had been killed. He'd come back yesterday in time for the funeral. Too late for Riley to see him first. He would find the time. Later.

At last, the service was over. Owen's parents came forward. They scraped up a handful of earth and tossed it into the grave. That was when his mother lost it. Wailing, inconsolable, she was led away by her husband and Mrs. Leaven from the village. The muscles around Riley's heart tightened. He felt their grief, every painful stab.

It fueled his fury.

None of this was right.

He knew a way to make it better.

But it would take time.

Those less acquainted with Owen stepped respectfully back to allow his family and friends nearer to the grave. More earth and flowers were thrown into the hole. Riley waited until almost the end. Owen had been his best friend, had been since they were four years old, but he waited. An unnatural feeling of calm imbued him. It was so different from the heightened emotional state he'd been in since the terrible news had hit. A tiny part of him was frightened by these feelings. Terrified.

But anger was a bigger emotion than fear and his lust for vengeance was greater still.

As he walked forward to throw a handful of earth into the hole, Riley watched Mark Hazard across the grave. Mark's opaque eyes stared into his. Time seemed frozen as they held each other. It was a devastating moment.

Something inside Riley shifted — a great impression of relief accompanied by a rush of fear — like a frightened child engulfed by the tide. He knew something with chilling certainty — Mark Hazard was the man who could change everything. No — would change everything.

As he stared into his eyes, he realized Mark was maybe thinking the exact same thing.

Sign up for our newsletter and find out about all our romance book releases, eBook sales and promotions, sneak peeks and FREE romance books!

About the Authors

L.M. Somerton

Lucinda lives in a small village in the English countryside, surrounded by rolling hills, cows and sheep. She started writing to fill time between jobs and is now firmly and unashamedly addicted.

She loves the English weather, especially the rain, and adores a thunderstorm. She loves good food, warm company and a crackling fire. She's fascinated by the psychology of relationships, especially between men, and her stories contain some subtle (and some not so subtle) leanings towards BDSM.

Cheryl Dragon

A lover of unusual things, Cheryl Dragon enjoys writing unique stories with sinfully hot erotic romance. She loves cats, coffee and book signings where she can meet her fans. Cheryl lives in the Chicagoland area.

Elizabeth Hollows

Elizabeth Hollows is an Australian writer of LGBT love stories specializing in homosexual or lesbian romance. Her preferred genres are fantasy, science fiction and contemporary/modern.

She has been writing since she was twelve, but has spent the last few years writing romance stories and discovering a passion for LGBT romance.

When Elizabeth is not writing she embroiders, reads and plots her next novel. She is a fan of the winter months and always has a book in her handbag and a cup of tea nearby.

These authors love to hear from readers. You can find their contact information, website details and author profile page at https://www.pride-publishing.com

www.ingramcontent.com/pod-product-compliance
Lightning Source LLC
Chambersburg PA
CBHW020422180626
46812CB00003B/1112